The Student Librarian

Written by
Victoria Lynn Osborne

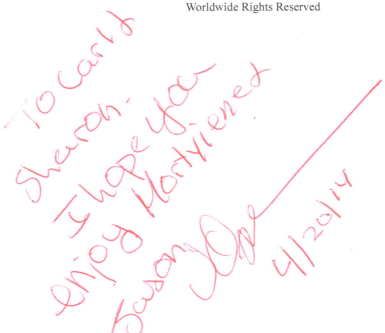

To Carld
Shearon.
I hope you
enjoy Mortimer!
Season

4/20/14

The Student Librarian

(A Jason & Mortyiene Mystery)

Written by Victoria Lynn Osborne

© Copyright 2013 – Worldwide Rights Reserved

FIRST EDITION

The Student Librarian is the first in the
Jason & Mortyiene Mystery series.

Editor-in-Chief: Steve William Laible

Cover Design: Stephanie Martin

Formatted for Publication: Vicky Rummel

Published by The Kodel Group, LLC
PO Box 38 - Grants Pass, Oregon 97528
KodelEmpire.com

Imprint: Empire Holdings

Library of Congress Control Number: 2013921909

Print ISBN 978-1-62485-019-6

eBook ISBN 978-1-62485-020-2

Blog: Goodreads.com (Victoria Osborne)

Printed in the United States of America, Europe, Asia and beyond...

To Frances Osborne
Thank you for everything.

Acknowledgements

There are so many people to thank for getting a debut novel ready for publication. First a thanks to Steve William Laible and the team at Kodel Group Publishing. If it wasn't for you this novel would not exist. Thanks also to Ruth, Jodi, Linda, Robin, Charlotte, Anne, Mnette, Cherie, Phyllis, and Vickie, the ladies of my writing groups. Without your valuable insight my novel might not be as strong. A special shout out to my cousin, Stephanie, for the amazing book cover. And special thanks to Frances, my mother, who created the environment needed to pound out this novel. And a finally thanks to you, gentle reader, for buying my book and falling in love With Jason and Mortyiene. May you enjoy many more tales of mystery with these two.

Prologue

The chill winter air burrowed through the off duty guard's heavy clothing. He bent his head over and pulled up the collar of his coat against the damp fingers of wind and sleet.

Behind him a shadow separated from the building gliding over muddy puddles and ruts in the road.

The cold of winter did not bother the shadow as it stalked its quarry. Passersby had their heads bowed to the rain and snow and did not notice the malevolent presence.

The guard turned down a side street, picking up his pace as his destination came into view.

Suddenly the shadow struck, jumping the hunched form of the guard from behind. A flash of fang sunk deep into the guard's neck. Blood flowed from two puncture wounds. It mingled with the mud, as the metallic smell filled the air. Its sharp tang was diluted by the rain and snow.

The shadow dragged him deeper into the alley. The guard's shirt plastered to his body with fresh blood and rain. His heels dug furrows in the mud as the shadow forced him deeper into the still darkness of the deserted street.

It was over so fast he was not able to cry out. Trails of blood washed down into the main street mingling with the mud and filth of the city. But the shadow was gone leaving only the faint smell of rotten eggs.

Chapter 1

Jason smacked parched lips, and adjusted his headgear, red from the persistent, irritating dust of the Red Rock Desert. He dismounted from his hardy desert bred horse. As dawn was breaking on the eastern horizon the rest of the caravan dismounted from their horses and camels. All around him was red sand, red rock, red mesas and red dust. Wind blew constantly, causing the sand to move in waves. He groaned and knocked more dust off his clothing and ran his fingers through his sandy brown hair. He turned to help unload the pack camels.

Jason, a twenty-four year old wizard, was on his way to The Library. This long desert trip was made by every magic user who progressed to the required complexity.

Back at home he was a detective for the Pegasus Cove constabulary and was assigned, last winter, to a murder that appeared to be a vampire kill. The investigation had been put on hold while he took classes at The Library.

As the sun rose on the eastern horizon Jason and the other students helped make camp. They set up the yurts that were enchanted to keep cool despite the inhumanely hot weather of the day. Even though it was still early spring the days would be unbearably hot.

Scarlet, a childhood friend of his with hair the color of her name, had a smattering of freckles on her creamy skin. She hitched up red robes between her legs and waded out into the middle of the spring.

"Kaccet cizezek." She muttered words of the incantation and water bubbled cold and clear around her feet, rising to her knees. The caravan guards and travelers filled up their water skins, gulping down the cool water. While Andee, the caravan sorcerer, cooled the earth beneath the yurts.

"Hrter Boris hrrinj jurumel'frr anr jurumelfrr genrlemrr revr'prr." Boris murmured. The beasts quieted under his soothing

voice.

Adelaydah helped with the cooking fires. She was of average height, not more than five foot eight, with long brown hair woven into a simple braid. Her purple robes designated her as an illusionist. Because her magic, at this time, would not be of much use, she helped out with the cooking and cleaning. However, her talents had been put to use during an invasion of her hometown when she crafted an illusion that saved herself and several children.

Soon the meal was cooking. The aroma of cooking meat caused Jason's stomach to rumble. It was cold traveling through the desert at night. But, soon after the morning broke and the sun beat down on the red desert, the temperatures were inhuman. The desert was always traveled at night. In another couple of months the desert would be impassable as the temperature would soar into triple digits even at midnight.

LaFlora, the lead guard of the caravan, was in a heated argument with Shang, a guard. Adelaydah glared at them as she moved to help serve the final meal before everyone retired.

"She was there," Shang hissed at LaFlora, oblivious to the watching students. "She remembers." His black hair fell into deep brown eyes. Muscles tensed under his bronze skin that was built for dealing with desert heat.

"So what if she does. We need to get past this or we will be stuck forever remembering that. She won't say anything she hasn't already said before. You need to return to your duties," LaFlora snapped at him. She grabbed her plate and started shoveling in food.

Adelaydah sat down next to Jason. She handed him a bowl of meat sweetened with dates and honey and a cup of chilled mint tea. "They're at it again." She leaned back against the yurt.

Jason nodded as Scarlet joined them. "I wonder what they are talking about." He loved mysteries it awakened the detective in him.

"You need to eat," Scarlet said, glaring. "The food is enchanted to help endure the heat, you know that."

Jason sighed and nibbled the food. "I will never get used to this food. If I didn't have to make this journey to The Library I would be home working on the murder last winter." He leaned back against the wall of the yurt.

Boris tended to the animals, taking them down for water now that the humans had replenished their own supplies. Boris was a massive man, with huge gnarled hands. Jason knew him from The Mountain, and that he was talented with Beast Magic. Farmers and even pet owners would bring their livestock to him for healing or help with breeding. He was gentle when tending the animals. His weather-beaten face was often times graced with a huge grin. Boris stopped by the fire and got his own huge bowl of food, a hunk of bread, a cup of mint tea, and lumbered to where the others were sitting.

Jason studied the animals, where they were staked. They browsed eating the scant rough grass near the spring along with hay and grain enchanted to allow them to endure the heat of the day.

Scarlet motioned to the guards that were still in a whispered shouting match. "I think that is going to be trouble," she muttered. "I knew LaFlora from when she was an officer in the army at Pegasus Cove. She was a friend of Daddy's and resigned shortly after you moved in," she said to Adelaydah.

Adelaydah shrugged and finished up her supper. She fiddled with her bowl and used a hunk of bread to get the last of the sauce sopped up. "I never knew her. But she does seem to be angry with the other one called Shang. I hear he is from these parts. That is why they hired him for this caravan."

Jason finished up his dinner the taste of goat, saffron, and dates lingering on his tongue and looked over the summoned water in the watering hole. "Here I'll take these." He reached for the bowls from Scarlet, Adelaydah and Boris. He scrubbed the bowls in the stale water bin, and let them air dry in the make shift kitchen. The sun climbed into the sky as he returned to his friends.

Jason yawned and stretched. "Time for bed. Once everyone is ready I'll turn off the lights." Around him other students and caravan travelers got ready for the day-time sleep. LaFlora posted guards for the caravan and she herself crawled into the soldiers yurt.

"Ready," a voice called.

"Lighlun nalh," Jason said. The light in the yurt dimmed as the dark spell filled the interior.

The request was echoed in several more shelters. Jason spent the next half hour or so bending the sunlight around the sleepers in their bedrolls giving them darkness that was deep, not pitch black, before he returned to his own yurt.

The yurts were cooled by sorcery that not only cooled the air but also the earth on which they rested. He crawled into his own bed roll and cast the spell, that plunged his sleeping area into night quality dark. He dry swallowed a pill to help him sleep. Tossing and turning her waited for the enchanted pill to allow sleep to take him.

* * *

The sun beat down on the yurt. Jason felt it, despite the cooling of the ground and the air. He stirred restless shoving his bedroll off his legs. He dreamt of a group of spell casters in black shot with red thread. Masked they chanted, in what looked to be a section of the library. *"Pox Shax xuixrix xax, Poxshax xhoxwrix xax, Poxshax xraxctrix xax xishx'x"* He could not make out the words, but the intent was clear. The chanters stood around a circle that gleamed with symbols.

A great portal opened and something came out, inhuman, beastly and terrifying. It had clawed feet, like that of a mutated bird, and a dove's head which peered without blinking. One baleful eye turned to him, and he heard its inhuman laughter echoing up through him.

"No!" he screamed. He bolted upright, his heart pounded. His small clothes were wet with sweat despite the cooled interior.

On other sleeping pallets the others rolled and muttered in their sleep. He waited a moment for his eyes to get used to the dim interior, then headed outside for some fresh air despite, the oppressive heat.

He couldn't breathe. He clawed at his throat as he stumbled out into the bright desert sun. The heat, after the cool dimness of the yurt, took his breath away. He struggled to breathe in the scorching air, blinking as he peered around the camp.

The heat and the light snapped him to full awareness. He stumbled to the spring warmed from the sun but still cool He stripped off his sky blue robes and dove into the water in just his small clothes. Sliding through the cool water and surfaced near the center of the sorcery made lake. As he treaded water he watched Shang approach LaFlora. The two began to fight again. LaFlora was taking her turn at watch. For the entire trip Jason watched the two of them fight. Curious about what had upset them so much, he swam closer.

At first they did not notice him and continued unabated.

"She was there. She saw us." Shang paced, his fingers clenching and unclenching.

"It does not matter if she had seen us," LaFlora hissed under her breath. "Keep your voice down. Or you will awaken the whole caravan. It is your sins that are being visited upon you. Though my hands are not clean of this either. When we finish getting the caravan to The Library, you will be released from your service to either sign up or return to your homelands."

LaFlora stopped and put her hand on Shang's arm, noticing Jason paddling nearby. "Do you need assistance student?" She said rose and strode toward the water.

Jason started to tread water, conscious of the fact that he was in his small clothes. "No Captain," he called back, light brown eyes dancing as he moved further out into the water. "Just a bad dream. I needed some air."

She headed back to her post and whispered some orders to Shang, who returned to the soldiers yurt.

Jason got out of the lake, shrugged into his robes, and headed back to the tent. He thought he could sleep without an enchanted pill, that the dip in the pool would be enough. He lay back, uncomfortable despite the cool interior, hoping that exhaustion would take him. Finally, he swallowed another enchanted sleeping pill and dreamless sleep enveloped him.

* * *

That night the caravan started its journey from Sebastian Oasis to Guriel well. The line of horses and camels spread out along the route. The air was still and even the dunes seemed to be still. He pushed his way through the thick night air fighting it every step of the way.

Scarlet rode up to him and whispered. "This is weird not natural. I think something is about to happen."

Jason kept his horse in pace with her. "What do you mean?" He whispered back.

"The air, the wind, it feels..." She paused looking around at the desolate landscape. "...unnatural."

Andee, the caravan sorcerer, pulled up his pony next to LaFlora. Jason spurred his horse a little closer to hear what they were saying.

"Captain," Andee's quiet voice was tinged with tension. "We need to stop and prepare."

"Don't overreact. There have been no signs of one. If there is then we will stop."

Jason and Scarlet's eyes met, their suspicions confirmed. Something was wrong.

Boris rode up. "The animals are restless," he said.

Jason looked back at the pack camels and horses their ears swiveled and their eyes rolled as they champed at their bits.

"Something big is coming. Scarlet says there is something wrong with the air." Jason whispered to Boris.

A guard yelled from the back of the caravan and ran toward the front. Jason looked behind him to see a huge wall of dust bearing down.

The captain turned in her saddle her eyes widened as she saw the sand storm blowing toward them. The wind howled. "Run," she yelled. "Get to that gap between the mesas. We need to put up a stone barrier," she screamed at the caravan sorcerer.

The members of the caravan spurred their horses and camels into a run. The animals jumped at the need to flee the huge storm. Jason gave his mount his head. They thundered toward the gap between the two mesas.

Scarlet and Andee led the charge as the caravan dashed through the gap. They leapt off their horses. On either side of the Gap, Andee and Scarlet put their hands against the mesas, chanting. *"Kock sovzceta sz'wakk."*

The mesas started to grow laterally, from their efforts, each one becoming wider and wider. Gravel, boulder, and rock disappeared from the nearby countryside absorbed by the wall as it began to grow.

Behind the wall Boris quieted the animals putting shields over the eyes and noses of the horses. The camels drew up in a circle their heads down.

Jason covered his face and eyes with his scarf and the other members of the caravan hid next to the rock wall that the sorcerers had summoned.

The wall groaned when the storm hit. Dust reared up roaring as it whipped the clothing of those in the caravan. Adelaydah grabbed Jason's hand and squeezed. Scarlet huddled on his other side. Boris sat a bit away singing a beast master's spell to the horses and camels.

The dust dug into Jason's clothing and working its way into his headgear and robs. The grains were sandpaper against his skin. The stars vanished concealed by a great black cloud of sand and debris. Everyone in the caravan huddled behind the sorcerers rock wall, waiting for the night air to still.

It seemed like hours before the howling wind stopped. Jason raised his eyes shaking dust and sand from his clothing. Scarlet and Adelaydah looked up as well. Everyone staggered to their feet.

"That storm," Scarlet whispered to Jason. "It did not feel natural. I know air and that air was ..." She paused a moment, "... malevolent."

"What do you mean?" Jason hissed. He noticed that Adelaydah looked scared.

"Something made the winds do that. It was not a natural storm."

"Dust storms happen all the time." Jason said trying to reassure his friend.

"Not like this. Trust me Jason there's a presence moving out there. It is changing the desert. Now the desert works against us. It wants us dead. You need to tell the captain."

Boris and the other caravan drivers tended the animals. They removed the shields that covered the eyes of the horses. The tack was removed as the drivers groomed the animals making sure no dust worked its way under the tack.

"I tell you captain," Andee said looking around, "That storm was not natural."

"Scarlet agrees." Jason said as he walked up to the captain and the caravan sorcerer. "She said the air was malevolent."

LaFlora looked at both of them. "There's not much I can do about it. We need to get to Guriel Well for the day. When we get to The Library we will see what they know about the strangeness of the desert."

The caravan crawled along the desert road again. It had taken awhile to calm the horses and to clean the sand or grit from under their tack. Jason looked at the eastern horizon, frowning. The dust storm had delayed their progress. Guriel Well was still a half a night's march.

LaFlora, sensing the need for speed, picked up the pace, leading the horses into a mile eating but spine jarring trot. They traveled in silence alternating between posting and sitting. The sun had climbed in the sky by the time the caravan arrived at Guriel Well.

The water of the natural well was brackish and clotted. Sandbars were formed along the edges of the spring. Scarlet studied the water. Her eyebrows knitted in concentration. She waded into the center of the well and said, *"kaccet cisezek"* She lifted her arms calling for the water to rise. The water remained shallow and brackish. The animals strained at their leads trying to get to the black water.

"Kaccet cisezek." Her voice rose in defiance. Andee stopped with his duties of cooling the ground beneath the erected yurts. He waded out to the well and joined her.

"I'm not sure what is going on," Scarlet told Andee. "It feels like the water is being held back. Do you think it has something to do with the dust storm?"

"Maybe," Andee replied. "Let me try. *Kaccet geccetz tzis sz'weck.*"

Water started to ooze from the red mud. When the well was filled it was still black looking but potable. The men and women of the caravan filled up their water bags and sat down to eat. While the horses and camels drank their fill.

Andee give his report to LaFlora. "That water was hard to call. We must get to The Library tomorrow. Something is working against us in the desert. I fear tomorrow night will be even worse."

Jason sat down to eat the cold rations that were provided as there was no time to cook before the sun was too hot. After a half hour putting out the lights in the different yurts. He stripped off his outer clothes, swallowed a sleeping pill and collapsed on his bed roll into a dreamless sleep.

The following night, they pushed their mounts harder. The red rock of the desert sent sparks glints off the horses shoeing.

LaFlora pulled up raising her hand. "Take fifteen minutes people. Make sure the horses are watered." She swung from her own roan horse and moved to the animals drinking water.

Boris swung off of his huge horse and got the horses water from the water bags.

Jason dismounted stretching his legs. He could feel saddle sores developing on his thighs.

In his mind he could hear his mother lecturing. "You've got to get used to riding. The trip to The Library is long. You will thank me later if you do practice riding."

Jason had dismissed her as overly worried. He rubbed the inside of his chapped legs and grimaced. Now he wished he had listened to her more carefully.

Scarlet excused herself and headed out into the brush to take care of her own business.

"Damn dust," Boris muttered, "It gets into everything even my bed roll."

Jason chuckled and checked the cinch on his saddle.

"Next," Scarlet said as she rejoined the group. Adelaydah slipped off and Scarlet worked on her own saddle.

A scream rang out across the scrub brush and sandy rocks.

"Adelaydah," Scarlet cried looking for her friend.

LaFlora drew her blade and charged into the brush the direction that Adelaydah took.

"Mouen nothal." Jason shouted. A sphere of light exploded from his fingers, surrounding himself and his friends.

Boris moved, with surprising grace for his size, to the animals calling to them in the deep rumbling voice of a beast master calming them. *"Jvrhor 'frr anr jvrrumel 'frr remrairn 'prr jararm."*

Four huge Scorpions swarmed the caravan, their massive pincers clicking in the night air. They were twelve feet long and their massive tails were curved over deformed heads.

"What the hell," Scarlet cried. Her fingers moving in the complex gestures of a sorcerer. "Something has disturbed them."

The scorpions advanced. Jason could see their stingers curled over their heads. They towered over LaFlora and the other guards who had formed phalanx in front of the students.

"Ckizback ackack gek ta'scozkatakz." Andee and Scarlet stood shoulder to shoulder calling out in unison. Two balls of fire roared out over the scorpions slamming into their alien bodies. The fire bounced off the chitinous armor and the scorpions continued to advance.

"Mouen voulun." Jason called. A pale blue ray zipped from his index finger and pierced the eye of a scorpion.

The beast reared up, striking blindly, its tail glancing off a guard's shield. Some of the others fell back pulling out their bows and letting arrows fly. LaFlora slashed at the tail of a scorpion. The stinger flew into the surrounding brush.

"Where's Shang." He yelled trying to be heard over the roar.

Another piercing scream rang from the brush surrounding the party. Adelaydah staggered toward her friend crying out a spell. *"Phreathenish thivershan'th xiez'x oth gianthf eathlh'th."* She stumbled tripping over the uneven ground as a giant bird erupted from her raised fingers. The roc triggered an instinct in the scorpions' limited brains and they backed off recognizing their natural predator. Scarlet rushed to her friend and dragging her to dubious safety behind the armored men and women.

LaFlora gave a Pegasus Cove battle cry. "Honor and duty above all else." She launched herself at the scorpion circling the spells casters.

"Mouen nothal," Jason reinforced the light shield around the group. The swirling lights distorted their location. He could see them reflecting in the many facets of the eyes and something else deep in them. An alien intelligence became clear to him.

Suddenly an eye sprouted a sword buried up to the hilt. Green ichor spewed and splashed on LaFlora's armor. The fluid clung to her armor causing it to sizzle and pop. LaFlora dropped to the sand. She rolled on it trying to scrub off the acidic ooze.

"Kaccet katzek." Scarlet twitched her hands and drew water from the only sources that had it, the tanks, bags, and people. A small raincloud formed over LaFlora. Water ran down her armor washing away the corrosive fluid.

As soon as it stopped sizzling Scarlet collapsed, her lips cracked and bleeding as she lay on the ground. Jason moved to stand over her as another fireball launched through the night and smashed into the scorpions.

The air was filled with the scent of scorpions on fire and their chittering screams echoed in his ears. Boris staggered from their painful cries. Jason saw him clinging to his horse trying to keep his footing as scorpions burned.

"Can you turn them away?" Jason yelled to the beast master.

"No," Boris yelled back, "I am barely able to speak to insects to begin with and these scorpions are enraged. I cannot get through to them."

"Mouen voulun," Jason said. Another light ray jumped from his index finger to pinpoint a gap in the scorpions armor.

Adelaydah crawled over to Scarlet grabbing her water and dribbling some between Scarlet's parched lips. She held her friend to her breast as she tried to get water down her.

LaFlora reached to her belt and pulled a vial popping the cap she drank it all in one shot. Blood streamed down her left arm. The armor was dented where pinchers had grabbed her. Wincing in pain, she returned to the fight.

"Ckizback ackack gek ta'scozktak." Andee screamed. A massive fireball flew from his hands streaking toward the remaining scorpions. He bellowed for LaFlora and the guards to move out of the way. It streaked starting in a pin point light of flame as the men and women of the guard dove back the scorpions, sensing the retreat, pressed forward and the explosion knocked the caravan off

of its feet. Camels and horses broke their leads and ran from the battle. With a strange lithe grace Boris leapt onto one of the horses as it thundered away.

When the smoke cleared the chitinous bodies of the scorpions were strewn among wounded guards, and discarded weapons. The water tanks and most of the water skins had lost their moisture. LaFlora's enameled armor was pockmarked and destroyed.

"Shang report!" LaFlora bellowed. No answering cry of acknowledgement. The guards and students remained silent. LaFlora charged off through the bushes ordering the rest of the soldiers to stand ready in case of more attacks.

Jason followed her hoping that he might be able to help her out while Adelaydah frantically looked for more water to rehydrate Scarlet. She kept squeezing the bags wringing out the last drops.

A short distance from the caravan they found him. His face bloated and blackened from scorpion venom. His fingers were wrapped around his blade looking like he was trying to draw it. His throat was swollen around a sting showing that the scorpion had a lucky shot.

LaFlora fell to her knees next to the man and tried to find a pulse, but, even Jason could see, that there was none. LaFlora looked up at Jason, her eyes were watering already. "He has been under my command before. He was a good soldier despite his transgressions."

Jason was tempted to ask what transgressions when he smelled the scent of rotting eggs. He looked around puzzled trying to find the sulfurous spring. "That smell, captain. Do you smell it?"

LaFlora took a tentative sniff. "The desert is full of sulfur springs. It probably had a lair close to one."

Something niggled at the back of Jason's mind about sulfur. He knelt next to the soldier and rummaged through his pouch. LaFlora glared at him and moved to stop him when Jason pulled out a note.

Shang:

I wish to welcome you back home to the tribes. We will be awaiting your return with great joy. It is our thought, that it is time to reclaim the great oasis from The Library. Your sword and your experience will speed us to our destiny. The Gods are with us in our holy crusade. For too long have we allowed the infidels to remain within our homeland. May the great lord Ishkatar grant us a swift victory upon the return of our most favored son of the desert.

For the honor of the desert

Sarad

Jason read the letter as LaFlora glared at him. "It was not your place to violate his privacy." She snatched the paper from him.

Jason stood up dusting his robes off. "I am a detective for Pegasus Cove constabulary, and this was not a natural attack. We were targeted. I believe that Shang was the main target. Boris was trying to reach the minds of the scorpions. He is not a hive master, but he does have some influence. He said that the scorpions were enraged. Furthermore the attack was timed for when Shang was not with the caravan. He was alone with his defenses greatly reduce. I am not sure where the closest sulfur springs are, but I do know they are not close enough for Scarlet to draw water from them that cleansed the corrosive blood from you. Furthermore, scorpion blood is not acidic so why was it corroding your armor. I believe that Shang was murdered, and this letter, well read it yourself. This letter gives us motive."

LaFlora studied the letter and as she read her lips pursed into a tight thin line, her left hand clenching and unclenching as she read on. "I can't believe this. No, he would not betray his people his duties."

"It sounds to me like he already has. I fear the LBI, Library Bureau of Investigations, will want to know what dishonor he brought to the soldiers of Pegasus Cove. They will ask you as his commanding officer what you know. I would think about the long running implications, if I were you. I leave the letter in your custody, but I am going to tell the peacekeepers that you have the letter so make sure it remains safe. It might help us find if he was killed, who killed him and why. As the letter, though it strongly implies, it does not conclusively prove that he was going to betray The Library. His family will still receive his pension I believe."

LaFlora looked at the letter and folded it up tucking it in her pouch. She reached down and swung the fallen man over her shoulder and returned to the caravan.

Boris had calmed the camels and horses and had returned to the caravan with them as well. Jason knelt beside the charred bodies of the four scorpions studying them, troubled.

"There is something wrong with them." Boris whispered as Jason returned to the caravan. "I wish I knew, perhaps the lab at The Library will know."

Jason nodded. "This is our last leg a lot of fodder and food has been used up. Lets pack up one of the carcasses so that the hive masters can look at it."

Boris straightened up a bit, "I am not sure. These scorpions just do not feel natural."

Jason and the others fed and watered the horses. The bright moon lit the way of the final leg of the journey to The Library, a small dot on the western horizon.

Chapter 2

Jason rode next to Scarlet as the caravan struggled on the last leg of the journey.

Scarlet was strapped to a camel, barely breathing. They made frequent stops to dribble small amounts of the remaining water into her mouth.

The desert changed as they rode. The rocky crimson hills and mesas were getting smaller. Gravel and pebbles were being ground into a fine red dust. The landscape went from a palette of reds and maroons down to endless dunes of dust and sand. The farther they rode toward the desert the flatter the land became.

"What is happening to the mountains and mesas?" Jason asked, urging his horse to keep pace with LaFlora.

"It's The Library," LaFlora said. "It steals the rock from around it to create new rooms."

Boris rode his horse up to LaFlora. "The animals need more water or they will die."

LaFlora called a halt, frowning as she studied the still dark horizon.

"Water the horses and camels," she ordered.

The caravan shuddered to a halt. Its member dismounted and tended the horses and camels. Boris and the caravan drover, ran fingers over the horses and camels checking for stress or dehydration in the animals.

"Riwrhr jahorfrr ryrenprfrr." Boris murmured. The animal lifted its head and rested it on Boris's shoulder. Its eyes clearing but still weak.

"Captain," he said, after he helped tend the animals. "How much farther?"

"Another three hours at least," she said.

"A couple of them won't make it," Boris said, if we continue to force them to carry packs."

LaFlora nodded. "What do you purpose we do?"

Jason drank a tiny sip from his water skin. The water was warm and tasted brackish remnants from the last oasis.

"Ok everyone, I need you to drop anything not needed. Bedrolls, yurts, everything. Leave it here on the ground we will pick it up later. We need to keep these animals going."

Jason dropped his bedroll and extra clothing. Jason ensured that his and Scarlet's supplies were well marked before he remounted his horse.

"Ok men," LaFlora commanded, "I need you to gather up the supplies and pile them over here. We will send for them when we get to the library." The drovers gathered up the gear and piled it in the middle of the red sand surrounding the pile with spells that would keep out the vermin of the desert.

Dawn broke in a panorama of red, blues, and yellows on the eastern horizon. The predawn cold was biting and Jason looked forward to the warmth behind the thick walls of the library. Sky Village, a tiny village huddled at the base of the massive library, beckoned them as they completed their journey.

The Library housed every book ever written in every dimension and time in its walls. The Library made a copy of every tome, grimmore, and book as the works came into being. As a result it was draining resources from the desert. When the desert was devoid of resource it would leech rock and building supplies from the mountains surrounding the desert and finally the continent itself. However, this would not happen for thousands of years. The rate at which The Library grew had slowed over the past millennium.

Jason's heart quickened. He fought the urge to run ahead. Scarlet remained unconscious as they drew closer to The Library. Even with extra water the animals still suffered. Their heads hung down and their tongues lolled out. The humps on the camels shrunk, and the horses tottered their heavy steps stirring up the fine red dust of the desert.

With the towering building growing closer and seeing the

huge stone wall, the horses picked up their pace. They knew the destination having made this trip before. Beyond the black iron gate was water and food, and they were as anxious to get to Sky Village as the rest of the caravan

Jason craned his head back as he entered through the gate into Sky Village, named because you could see the sky something that was hard to do in The Library.

Beneath the surface in deep caverns was the Gloaming. It spread under the continents and had its own cultures and people. Thousands of years ago the dwarves had excavated the great cavern, and called it the Gloaming. Jason knew that deep beneath the surface was another village known simply as Root Village. So named because it squatted at the roots of the library.

In the town square of Sky Village the students and guards dismounted at the Red Rock Caravan Company office. Stable hands darted out to tend the animals. Boris gave his horse a final pat, and stretched his legs out. Jason breathed in the scent of horses and camels as he dismounted.

Two peacekeepers, guards for The Library, were summoned to take Scarlet to the hospital wing. They eased her onto a stretcher and covered her with a blanket and trotted toward The Library with the still unconscious Scarlet.

A stable boy brought Jason water. "I'm Devario," he said, handing a skin of water to Jason. "You need to sip it or you'll get cramps."

Jason took shallow sips of the warm water. Boris and Adelaydah followed his example.

Tired and worn, Jason thought that he would never get all the dust out of the cracks and crevices of his body, where no dust had a right to be. He paused for a moment waiting for his friends to catch up They headed into The Library.

* * *

Passing through the massive double doors which stood sentinel a huge bell tolled. He looked up trying to identify the sounds and his gaze fell upon the statue of the Goddess Levet. As always her sad face gazed out over men and women that visited her domain. Adelaydah and Boris chatted apparently unaware of the bell. Jason paused and glanced around, visitors and students milled in the entry court. A couple of library cats, snoozing away on the most comfortable chairs in the area, glanced up at the door. The librarians paused in their work and looked at the entry then quickly returned to their work. After the red of the desert the shades of green and blue was a welcome change. The tables were made from warm golden oak. Brightly colored carpet, woven by the local nomads, graced the red stone floor.

"Come on," Adelaydah groaned. "Let's get done with registration and go to our rooms I need a shower."

Jason nodded. He snaked his way through throng of people. Brown robed librarians, blue robed wizards, and a rainbow of other adornments. He strode to where the wizards checked in. He could see Adelaydah checking in with the illusionist depart. Boris lumbered toward the beast master department as well. Scarlet would register with the sorcerers when she awoke.

The librarian looked up as Jason approached, "Greetings," he said eyeing him with a twinkle, "name please."

"Jason," he replied, "Jason Litwieler."

"Welcome Jason, I am Tighe," he replied. "Ah yes, here you are on the list. We were expecting you earlier in the night, but I hear you ran into some trouble with a few scorpions."

Jason nodded. "My friend Scarlet nearly died summoning water to save the captain. She is in the hospital wing at the moment. I will drop by to see her after I am settled in."

"We have the best healers, outside of The Cloud, here in The Library. I'm sure she is ok." Tighe handed Jason a sheaf of printed papers. "Here is your room assignment and class schedule. I hear you went through school in The Mountain with your friends so we have kept you together as much as possible." He studied Jason a bit longer, and leaned forward and whispered, "I am not suppose to ask this, but did you hear a bell when you entered the building?"

Jason nodded. "Yes. It was loud, but most of the people did not seem to react. What does it mean?"

Tighe leaned back in his chair, "you will find out soon enough, and let me be the first to say congratulations for making it to The Library. I am sure your time here will be most interesting." With that he laughed as Jason returned to his friends holding the paperwork that had his room number on it.

A cool breeze enveloped him, or what felt like one. He stopped at the entry to the upper rooms and looked around. She came into sight gliding like a pale shadow. She paused at the top of the stairs and looked around Straight raven black hair hung down to her ankles in a long braid. Skin tight black robes shot with metallic black and silver thread wrapped around her body, and flared out mid thigh cascading to the floor. Black piercing eyes peered out from her calm face. Alabaster skin glowed with an unearthly light. While red lips graced her lovely mouth of even white teeth.

Jason stopped and stared. Mortyiene was here at the same time. She was with them in The Mountain. He thought he would never look upon her again, yet here she was in The Library.
Boris saw him pause and followed his gaze. "She is way out of your league wizard boy," he laughed.

"I know, but there is something about her."

Adelaydah snorted, "Yes. Like she is the daughter of a military caste officer in Eversphere, the mortal enemy of the River's Alliance, if I must remind you. You know that city was responsible for the attacks on my village that killed everyone in it save for a few kids and myself."

Jason winced and turned his attention back to his friends. "You're right of course." He sighed and headed through the door to his rooms. Boris and Adelaydah followed close behind.

He paused one more time and looked over the hall full of

students. Mortyiene swept to the necromancy section with her friend Rhyann. LaFlora was arguing with a huge northman. His braided hair and beard sporting beads of rank and achievement. Why is LaFlora fighting with the man. He shrugged and headed up to his room eager to bathe after the long hot trip.

* * *

Mortyiene stretched out on a luxurious red sofa in her rooms. Hand carved mahogany and red furniture and great thick carpets woven in reds and golds decorated her suite. A huge fire roared in the fireplace bathing the room in warmth. Tall bookcases lined one wall and were filled with a variety of titles, including, surprisingly, a book on Wizardry. A bowl of fresh oranges and dates rested on the table. Two doors led off from the main living space, one to a bed chamber with a huge mahogany four poster bed with a crimson quilt. A fire sparked and sputtered in another grate its smoky scent filled the room with the pleasing odor of mesquite and pine smoke. The other door opened onto an plumbed bathroom with a great huge tub so deep she could float it in it. The accommodations would serve while she was at The Library.

She inspected the wardrobe and noted that her clothing was put away. A knock on the door interrupted her musing.

Rhyann was on the other side of the door. The vampiress looked resplendent in black robes. Rhyann's shoulder length wavy brown hair set off her pale glowing skin "I was headed down to Root Village for dinner and thought I would see walk with you to the lifts, if you are ready to go.

Mortyiene nodded, and quickly pinned up her braid in a loose bun. She liked having it high and up, and often times wanted to cut it. But hair was a symbol of your caste and rank in Eversphere, and the work required to keep her plaits that long indicated she was a woman of high rank.

"I'll be going up to the student dining room. I want to see who is here from the other side. It is not often I get to rub shoulders with the citizens of the River's Alliance I am always curious. I will walk with you to the lifts though. Enjoy Root Village"

Rhyann chuckled. "Well Mistress, don't get too fond of the light."

"Never." They walked to the end of the corridor and waited for the enchanted lifts. The doors slid open and Mortyiene suppressed an inward groan. "Greetings Lucero," she said catching the smirk on the vampiress face as Rhyann waited for the next lift going down.

"Heading for dinner as well Mistress?" Lucero moved back to allow Mortyiene entry.

"I will catch the next one," Rhyann said. She smiled and showed fang. "Nothing edible for me in the student cafeteria. You two have fun."

Mortyiene nodded and entered the lift sharing the ride with him. It wasn't that he was a bad sort. He was from a merchanting family and was struggling to be accepted into the caste of magic users. She knew her government assigned him to keep an eye on her and out of the clutches of the River's alliance and their talk of freedom.

The scents of fresh baked bread and cooked meat tickled her senses. She had grown weary of the rations of the Gloaming. However, the deep caverns of the earth were the domain of Eversphere and her allies and she was stuck eating what was available. She missed the open sky and fresh air on her journey.

Mortyiene thought back to the trip through The Gloaming. The first leg of the journey had been uneventful. The Gloaming was well civilized and the great cities of the dwarves were occupied by Eversphere and their allies. The problems came with the Black Sea.

The caravan had stopped for the night at Deep Port, the former dwarven city of Turrac Sul. The next morning they boarded the ship, Robber's Revenge and headed across the massive underground sea. Mortyiene had her own cabin in the forecastle, while her companions bunked together in the hold.

An underground storm had blown up. The deep tunnels and wide spaces generated weather. The man in the crow's nest called a warning to crew and passengers.

"All hands on deck." The first mate yelled. "We need to furrow the sails."

Sailors, soldiers and students rushed to the great masts and pulled in the sails, Mortyiene included. She threw her back into the task of folding the great sheets of canvas that propelled the ship.

The storm tossed the ship. Great waves crashed over the bow and swept barrels ropes and a couple of sailors into the choppy water.

Mortyiene huddled in her cabin during the storm clutching a pot in her hands and the taste of vomit stung her throat. She tried to lay down but the motion of the boat caused her to vomit even more.

The sea was connect by deep caves to the oceans above it. Water flowed down and with capillary pressure pushed up into the great basin. The ceiling was so high over the sea that it was impossible to see it. The light on the star board and port running boards shimmered wanly in the night.

Finally the seas calmed. Mortyiene stomach stopped rolling and she curled up on her bed and attempted to get some sleep. In a strange quirk the storm blew them ahead of schedule but that was not the terrifying part.

A dim elf, a race of subterranean elves with coal black skin and red eyes, climbed into the crow's nest and blew his horn. "Sea serpent dead ahead."

The sailors and soldiers swarmed onto the deck.

Mortyiene saw the serpent streak toward the small ship. "Crap," she swore.

She closed her eyes and set out black tendrils of magic to comb through the water looking for unclaimed dead. Nothing within range of her limited abilities. The most she could do was some small spells that would weaken the sea serpent.

"Szaiszes seszenshvias," she called. A poisonous green ray shot from her hands and struck the serpent's body. It glowed the same color for a moment or two then faded.

The beast brought its triangular head level with the deck and shot over the main body of the ship. The scaly green body wrapping around the hull.

The timbers groaned from pressure as the serpent wrapped around the ship a second time. If the beast started to tighten, they would find themselves adrift in flotsam.

Mortyiene targeted the serpent with another poisonous green ray to drain the energy from the beast. The sea serpent showed signs of weakening.

Rhyann, the vampiress, surged forward claws and fangs extended. The vampiress' inhuman strength tore at the scaly body sliding along the deck. Sea green blood flowed from the beasts body where ever Rhyann struck.

Lucero knelt beside Mortyiene. He drew a circle in chalk and was inscribing it with symbols.

The guards and the crew flew at the serpent swords drawn and hacking at it. Their weapons doing some damage but not much. The triangular head appeared again on the port side of the ship and shot over the deck. The serpent now had three coils wrapped around the small ship.

"What are you trying to do?" Mortyiene yelled to Lucero.

"I'm trying to displace the ship. It is complex magic. I lack the proper words, but we need to get the ship out of the coils." He yelled back.

Rangers and soldiers stood on the upper deck of the aftercastle. They strung their bows and let loose their arrows. Black arrows rained down on the body bouncing off of the scaly hide.

Not one damn offensive spell caster on this whole ship.

Mortyiene thought as she cast another draining ray.

One of the rangers, an older man with thickly gnarled hands and well defined biceps shot an arrow that sprouted from the beast's eye. A fountain of sea green blood spewed from the perforated socket.

The serpent roared and loosened its coils. The sea churned near the ship. Lucero finished his circle and activated it. The ship shimmered and reappeared ten yards from the sea serpent's coils.

"To the oars you sea dogs. Pull for your life," the captain bellowed. Sailors and students swarmed for the oars.

Mortyiene knew she was exempt, and stood on the aft section of the ship.

The sea serpent continued to thrash in pain as the sea churned with foam. The sails filled with an errant gust. The oars pulled through the water. The ship picked up speed sailing in full sale in front of the wind with the oars making it go even faster.

A few hours later the twinkling lights of Ranger's Roost appeared, the last town of civilization until Root Village. They had arrived two full days ahead of schedule. The ship, injured though she was, had made good time. The captain ordered oars for the remainder of the journey with the crew working in shifts.

Mortyiene had never been so happy to have both feet on the ground. She shook her head, trying to forget the journey and headed up to the cafeteria with Lucero.

Lucero wrinkled his nose at the food choices. However, she heaped up fresh salad greens and tomatoes on her plate, and speared a couple slices of roast beef, and a fresh baked potato.

Mortyiene heard the sound of laughing and followed it to a table. Her face warmed as she spied the man with sandy brown hair and dancing eyes. He was with his friends, a burly beast master, and the dark haired illusionist. She heard, in the entry hall, that the sorceress was still in the hospital wing. She remembered Jason from the mountain. An instructor assigned them to work as partners. She had never worked so well.

Lucero followed her gaze to the table. He tried to steer her to the other side of the room. She feigned oblivion to his treaties and headed to the table next to Jason and his friends. She wanted to catch up on the gossip. Maybe she would overhear something good.

"I still think it is murder," Jason whispered

Mortyiene barely heard him over the sounds in the cafeteria. Murder! Her heart jumped at that word. Who was murdered and why? Her heart beat throbbed in her throat. Lucero frowned and said something to her. She dismissed what he was saying, she feigned concentration on cutting her roast. Her eyes pleaded with him to remain quiet.

Boris nodded his agreement with Jason. "Those scorpions did not feel right. But, insects and arachnids are hard on me. I do not talk to them well."

Jason sneezed into a handkerchief. "Damn cats," he muttered.

"I found a note," Jason whispered. "It said the nomads were planning on attacking The Great Oasis. Do you think the scorpion attack had something to do with that?"

Mortyiene held her breath. The nomads wanted to take over The Great Oasis?

Lucero rapped the table in front of her. "Mistress, you need to finish you dinner and return to your rooms."

The other table grew quiet and looked at the two of them. Mortyiene could have throttled Lucero at that moment. She knew he was angry with her for sitting close to the students from Pegasus Cove, and she knew why. Lucero's whole family would be killed in a bloody fashion if she left Eversphere. Even her own family could suffer. Her father's rank and prestige would keep most of her family safe. Lucero's family was expendable.

She sighed in resignation and finished her dinner. The roast and greens had lost their flavor.

The four students from Pegasus Cove finished their meals and took the trays to the scullery room. Mortyiene finished her meal in silence across the table from a glaring Lucero.

* * *

The night had flowed over Sky Village. Sounds of drinking and music spilled out into the night streets. Crickets chirped in the huge fields surrounding the school. When a shadow, blacker than the deepest recesses of the town, glided on to the street. Wrapped in the shadow a figure with glowing white skin and two piercing eyes studied the street looking for its quarry.

Yule was a big man, huge even. He walked home from Sky Inn, the only tavern in Sky Village. He was off duty, his braided hair and beard free from the encumbrance of armor or a helmet. An axe was belted at his waist. He was from the north and was built for cold not for heat. Beads of perspiration dotted his forehead. He was heading back to the Red Rock Caravan company and bunk for the night when the black shadow fell upon him.

The shadow moved so fast he had no time to scream or react. Fangs slid into his neck. Blood ran down his chest soaking his linen shirt. He struggled against a hand clamped firmly over his mouth. His heart fluttered in his chest as his life force drained away.

His heart beat stilled, and he was dropped to the dusty ground.

The shadowy being wiped its mouth and disappeared into the night leaving nothing behind but the drained man and a faint smell of rotten eggs.

Chapter 3

The next day the cafeteria was abuzz as Jason and his friends entered to have breakfast. "A guard died last night," Adelaydah said as she rubbed her temples.

Jason lifted a fork full of eggs and potatoes to his mouth. He gazed at her concerned. "Do you have a headache?"

Adelaydah nodded. "I think from dehydration. I cannot drink enough water."

Scarlet had been released from the hospital the night before and was eating a plate piled high with eggs, sausages and flapjacks. "He too was in LaFlora's squad," she mumbled through her stuffed mouth.

"Scarlet," Adelaydah chided. "You should not talk with your mouth full."

Scarlet finished her meal and drank some coffee, a luxury that The Library enjoyed as it was bordered on some of the best coffee plantations in the world.

"I hate it when my sorcery drains my reserves. Not sure if saving LaFlora was the right thing to do." Scarlet said, her mouth full of eggs and potatoes.

"I hear this time it was a vampire attack." Adelaydah pushed the food around on her plate.

A loud snort greeted that comment from the table next to them. "What makes you say that?" Mortyiene said her voice hushed. It seemed like the whole world held its breath when she spoke.

"Two puncture marks drained of blood. It sounds like a vampire to me," Adelaydah snapped back.

"We can't make assumptions Adelaydah. Just because Rhyann is responsible for the deaths in your village, does not mean that she is responsible for the death of the guard. There could be another explanation."

"I do not understand why she is allowed here at all. Shouldn't the peacekeepers arrest her and send her back to Pegasus Cove for trial?"

"What happens at the war must be dealt with away from the schools." Mortyiene glared at Adelaydah. "The schools' integrities must be preserved. If the war was brought to the schools then no one would advance." She stood suddenly, grabbing her tray and heading for the scullery. "Best you remember that Illusionist. This peace is all that keeps you safe."

Jason stood up when he finished his breakfast. He knew Scarlet, Adelaydah and Boris had classes in the morning. His first class, linguistics, was at a later hour. Curious, he headed out to Sky Village to look at the crime scene.

Yule's body had been taken to the morgue for examination by the healers and the little bit of blood left was quickly being absorbed by the red dirt that permeated the village.

He knelt down and shifted his vision to see residual magic. *"Oluhjallhau Jason l'yloolaulaylunloo la wallenun lath mouenun."*

The hard-packed earth shimmered before him with an overwhelming presence of black magic. So dark, but oddly with a faint undercurrent of red. It could be the heat from the rocks, he thought. The magic was cool and hot at the same time. He knelt studying the fading aura

"Anything interesting?" a cool voice said behind him.

Jason leapt to his feet his heart pounding in his chest. He turned to see Mortyiene watching him. "It is odd, though there is a lot of black energy which would make sense if indeed Rhyann did attack Yule. But it doesn't feel right. The light doesn't match."

"Rhyann is hundreds of years old. She knows the importance of the laws of peacekeeping for this area. It does not make sense that she would violate them," Jason continued.

"That is the first intelligent thing I have heard from your table." Mortyiene moved to stand next to him. His heart fluttered in his chest as he took in her subtle musky scent with a faint undertone of Hawthorne.

Mortyiene pointed out two footprints in the dust heading into an alley. "Look, I wonder where they are going." They traced the foot prints to a yellow powder circle in the dust with strange symbols traced in the same powder.

"Do you recognize them?" Jason asked.

Mortyiene knelt down beside the circle. "No, it is not something I am familiar with. Do you recognize it?"

"Wizardry does not use circles. Our magic is not that formal. Enchanters use circles but their circles radiate a gray light. This circle is radiating a deep black energy. However, there are more undertones of red here." He sighed. "These murders make no sense," he said willing his color vision off.

"Murders?' Mortyiene stood up from the inspection of the circle.

Jason nodded. "On the way here another guard was killed. He too was in LaFlora's squad and was fighting with her."

From the temple of Levet a bell tolled the hours. Jason swore, "Crap I need to go to class." He charged away from Mortyiene and headed back to The Library.

* * *

Jason ran his fingers along the spines of the Wizardry book. This section of the library had blue toned rugs gracing the red rock floors and the high narrow windows that looked over the desert were paned in glass of various shades of blue. He was studying the titles of the wizardry books when he first spotted her. He looked up briefly and, from the corner of his eye, saw a small black and white tuxedo cat seated on a chair.

He ignored her, other than taking out a handkerchief to cover his sneezing and went on looking at the books. He had been assigned a lesson in vocabulary and was in the wizarding section to learn new words.

Two aisles over he found the book he was looking for and

headed off in search of a study carrel. He found one tucked away in a corner. A rare blue paned window over looked the desert. The same black and white cat sat on the desk.

"It took you long enough," the cat said, looking steadily into his eyes.

Jason nearly dropped his books in surprise. "You can talk?" His mouth forming an O of surprise.

"Only to a few, I'm Edwardynah. It is nice to meet you." She sat on the desk, looking him up and down.

"Nice to meet you too. Now if you would be so good as to leave. You see, I am very allergic to cats." He emphasized this with a honk into his handkerchief.

"Sorry. I can't do that. You see I am your library cat."

"I know you are a library cat and, as you can plainly see, I am not a librarian. I am a student, and a detective for Pegasus Cove Constabulary. I think you have me confused with someone else."

Jason thought that if a cat could look even more irritated than normal this one surely looked that way. She sat up straight, her tail twitching and her ears swiveled back.

"Don't be dense Jason. You can talk to me. Hence you are a librarian."

Jason put his books down on the desk of the carrel. "I don't want to be a librarian. I am very happy in my current job. I just came here because I advanced enough to have the next level of spells opened for me."

Edwardynah leapt from the desk and wound herself around Jason's ankles. "I see that you are going to need proof. Come on I will show you your new rooms. If you are a librarian, the door will open to your touch. Since, apparently, talking cats are not enough to convince you."

Jason shot a regretful look at the quiet carrel, grabbed his books and followed Edwardynah deeper into the stacks.

* * *

As Edwardynah led him deeper into the stacks other cats looked up, amused at their passage. Sometimes he could hear what sounded like laughter rolled up in a purr. "Why are they so happy?" he asked.

"Because I'm saddled with you. They find it amusing. My last librarian, well he was much more into indulging my whims. I fear that I will be reminding you to feed me and clean my litter box." She paused for a moment and was quiet.

"Do you miss him?" Jason asked, stunned by the cat's sudden quiet.

"None of your business," she said. "This is the main entrance to your rooms and office. Do you see the lettering up there?"

Jason nodded looking above the carved oak entrance. It was a beautiful door inlaid with various textures of wood and carvings depicting shelves in a library and a cat sleeping in them. The spines of the books had different titles, like "Puss in boots," and "Of Mice and Men". The lettering over the door said, Investigator's Office."

"The last librarian had this door commissioned," the cat explained. "It is the only one like it in The Library."

Jason ran his fingers over the beautifully etched door. "Is this you?" he asked indicating the cat carved in relief on the door.

"I suppose so, but truly it is more of a tribute to all of The Library cats and our duties. We keep the scroll shrews in check. Go ahead. Open the door. If you are meant to be in this room, it will open at your touch."

Jason put his hand on the latch. It lifted easily, sliding open on well-oiled hinges. Inside the room took his breath away. A fireplace laid with wood graced the side of a large room. A deep blue sofa and two chairs beckoned in comforting warmth. Five doors led off of the room. Four were beautiful golden oak. The fifth was iron-bound dark mahogany.

"This is my home?" he whispered, walking into the room with deep richly textured carpet from the local nomads.

Edwardynah jumped up on one of the chairs and sat looking at him. "Actually it is my home. I am letting you stay here."

"I never had a cat, growing up." Jason glared at her. "I never knew what a pain in the ass you guys are."

Purring, Edwardynah curled up. "We are easy to take care of. Just give us everything we want and you will be happy. Lucky our needs are few-- a clean bowl of water, a full food dish, and fresh litter and we are happy." She rolled in the chair her paws waving in the air as she purred happily.

She jumped off of the chair and went to the first door. "This is your office where you will conduct most of your business."

Jason opened the door and peered inside at the heavy oak desk and he noticed that the bookshelves in the office had three books on it, two on illusions and one on thaumaturgy. Jason ran his fingers over the spines. Thick blue carpets covered the red rock of the floor and heavy blue drapes graced the large window that overlooked the fields surrounding Sky Village.

"This is your bedroom. We have taken the liberty of bringing your robes and belongings here. I would suggest that you send word to your parents that you wish the rest of your things sent here." Edwardynah nosed a door open directly across from his office.

"This room is your own private bathroom. Not every librarian gets their own. Most have communal bathrooms, but you are the Investigator. With that comes special privileges."

"The investigator?" Jason paused, stunned. "You mean I will be working on the most complex cases in the world?"

Edwardynah golden slitted eyes looked at him knowingly. "With insight like that, you will go far. Yes, from what I know of you, you have an aptitude for case solving. Have you ever wondered why it came so easily?"

Jason remembered his partner, a senior constable in Pegasus Cove. He had commented on how easily Jason picked up detecting.

"Yes," he said. "It was like second nature to me."

"That's The Library for you," Edwardynah said.

"But how did it know?" Jason asked, fingering the bed curtains on his huge bed.

"The Library has no sense of time. It brings the people it wants here, both magic users and non-magic users alike."

She paused before the last oak door. "This is your kitchen. Not much here. You are expected to take most of your meals in the cafeteria with other librarians and students. But occasionally you will eat in your rooms."

Jason moved to the last door. "Where does this one go?"

Edwardynah paused. "Do you know what an investigator does?"

"Not really. I know they solve complex crimes in and around The Library. Not much past that."

"Investigators cross the disciplines. They can go into places no one else can, including other librarians. Even here the disciplines keep strict separation. A wizardry librarian that ventures into the world of necromancy might not return in one piece. A hive master that goes to the sorcery section might come back singed. But you, Jason-- you are The Investigator. When you have finished speaking to the head of the bureau you will be able to go anywhere and research anything."

Jason opened the door. It was darker than his room, torches sputtered to life, revealing a staircase that twisted down into inky black depths.

Jason started down the stairs. One hand on the wall, the other on the spiral pillar and walked deeper into The Library depths. Though it only felt like three stories, he had the impression of immense depth into the earth. At the foot of the stairs was another iron bound door.

"Oluhjlhau wallenun mouen" he whispered, opening his sight.

The blackness of the energy hit him. He smelled rotting flesh and death. He pushed it open and found himself in the depths of The Library. Huge cobwebs hung from the black ceiling. Spiders skittered in the deep recesses. A skeletal cat paused midstride, a skeletal scroll shrew dangling from its mouth.

"Greetings librarian," it hissed softly. There was no breath in its bony body. "If I had not seen you come out, I would not know that you were a librarian. You should wear your robes. It would be safer. I will let Bli know there is a new librarian here."

Edwardynah sat on the stoop behind the door. "No thanks," she said to Jason's inquiring look. "And it is right, you should put on your librarian robes before wandering about down here."

"I'll just be a moment, not that long." Jason stepped into the moldy smelling stacks of necromancy. He ran his fingers along the spines of the books as dust rose from the cases. They don't believe in housekeeping down here he thought to himself.

The room was immense. A labyrinth of books beckoned him ever deeper. He saw a few more skeletal cats, but didn't sneeze, despite the extra dust. No fur, he thought. I wonder of Edwardynah would allow herself to be shaved. Naw, probably not.

Jason rounded a corner and stumbled on three necromancers in black robes. They were deep in conference and were not aware of him at first. The leader stopped talking and turned toward Jason. The necromancers wrinkled face wore lines of age and wisdom as he studied Jason.

"You do not belong here," the leader said raising his hands he started to cast a spell. Soon the other two added their spells and voices.

"Sish shiz shoushshaz szaishzes she wizarzvias os sifeshaz" The black robed figure reached out his fingers brushing along Jason robes. A deep cold settled into Jason's arm as the touch chilled him to the bone.

"Shinzvias os seazshas azzashzes she wizarvias." The woman's voice filled Jason with terror. A black wind smelling fetid and diseased whirled toward him. Every time he exhaled he felt his life-force drawn from his body and sink into the swirling maelstrom of decay.

"ʃ'ghuazdvias os she sisrazy savves she wizarvias." As the third necromancer called out. Jason heard skeletons shuffling toward the call of the necromancer.

"I'm a librarian," he yelped darting out of the way of the spells. He retreated down the aisle between the book cases.

"You don't look like one. Where are you robes?" the woman demanded, raising her hands in preparation for another spell."

"szaiszes sifeshaz." hissed the leader, the one that had touched him with the chill touch spell. A poisonous green ray burst from his index finger hitting Jason square in the chest.

Jason nearly crumbled to his knees as the strength was siphoned from him. He slumped against the bookcase, using it for a support.

"Skeletons attack the wizard," the third necromancer cried, as the dead things reached for Jason with boney fingers.

Jason shouted, *"Mouen Nothau."* A sphere of light sprung up about him shimmering in rainbow colors. Another poisonous green ray shattered upon his light shield refracting into pieces as the light absorbed it.

Jason turned. He raced down the corridor, glad he remembered his way down into the black depths. It seemed like the stacks were closing in on him. Spiders moved in webs above him. Skeletal with eyes of eerie red flame, attacked him with lumbering swings. He hit the door to his rooms at a run, flinging it open as he dived through. The door slammed shut behind him. He leaned on the rail panting for breath.

Edwardynah sat on the landing behind him her tail wrapped neatly about her paws. "Next time wear your robes," was all she said, as she turned and daintily made her way back up the stairs.

Jason followed, his heart pounding in his chest, and headed for his rooms. He took out a brown over-robe of a Librarian. The over-robe was sleeveless with high slits up both side seams and the front. His sky blue wizardry robes were worn underneath showing all that he was not only a librarian but a wizard as well. He had not seen brown robes on the necromancers that had attacked him, so he figured they were visitors.

"Neutrality is tentative. They have a right to protect their secrets," Edwardynah said. as her eyes followed him from her perch on his bed.

Jason was getting ready to go to his kitchen for a snack when a knock on the door interrupted him. Opening the door he saw a librarian.

"Good day. I am Barnabas. Librarian Laurel wants you in her office right now."

Baranabas, having delivered his message, quickly made his way back through the Wizardry section.. Jason grabbed his satchel and headed through the stacks to the main bureau floor.

The enchanted lift carried him without difficulty to the floor and Jason threaded his way through the maze of desks and smaller offices until he found Laurel's name

He knocked on a plain wood door with Laurel Penquite engraved on a brass plague attached to the door. "Come in," said a woman's clear strong voice from the other side of the door.

Jason entered, and surveyed the room. Sitting at a huge oak desk was an older woman. Her with gray hair caught up in a messy bun with two enchanted pens sticking out at odd angles. Her chocolate colored robes looked disheveled. Under the librarian over-robes was the sky blue of wizardry.

Across from her sat a tall skeletal man. He had no skin, and his eyes glowed with an unearthly red light. Bony fingers gripped the arms of his of the plain functional chair where he sat. He wore black under robes and brown librarian robes.

"You must be Jason," the wizard said, standing to shake his hand. Her grip was warm and firm, and Jason took an instant liking to her. "I'm Laurel, the head of the LBI. This is Bli. He is registering a complaint that the latest investigator was another wizard."

"Bli," Jason said, "Mortyiene mentioned you when I was at the crime scene. She said you are head of the Necromancy section and have been the librarian there for over two thousand years."

The librarian turned his flame red eyes to him and regarded him. The unearthly stare caused Jason's skin to crawl. Bli turned his attention back to Laurel. His strange eyes flared up. "This is unacceptable. It was time for another discipline. I will not allow this to go unchallenged." His voice was dry and raspy and devoid of all emotion.

"Bli," Laurel stood her ground glaring at the liche. "The choice is not mine, it is The Library's. Would you have me go against the will of that which we both serve?"

Bli stood dwarfing Jason with his towering presence. Waves of ancient black magic rolled off him. "At least assign him a partner, a partner from my discipline."

"That was my intention, which is why I asked you to come to my office. Do you have a candidate in mind?"

"As a matter of fact I do," There was another knock on the door, "and here she is now." Bli said sitting down and crossing his legs.

"Come in," Laurel's voice was apprehensive. She motioned Jason to the other seat in the office.

Jason sat his eyes glued to the door. His palms were sweating and his heart hammered in his chest. He felt his world lurch when Mortyiene glided through the door.

"Him!" her voice was tinged with shock.

"Her!" Jason jumped to his feet and clutched the back of the chair.

Bli gave a raspy chuckle. "Who else? They are of the same age. They shared classes at The Mountain so they are familiar with each other. She is well bred and educated. He is coarse and a bit crude. I have foreseen that the two of them will perform great acts together."

"Librarian Bli." Mortyiene choked out the name. "I cannot work in The Library. Eversphere won't allow it. I must return to my family."

Bli handed her a parchment. "Here is a letter with my seal on it. You have been assigned to the LBI. It has been acknowledged by the second administrator. Only the Uver himself is able to override it."

Mortyiene's hands trembled as she took the paper. "Why me?"

"You are smart, capable, and you and this man," he indicated Jason, "seem to have a bond of some kind. It is decided. You will remain here as an LBI adjunct agent, provided Librarian Laurel agrees."

Laurel sat at her desk, her hands steepled. "You know Bli, I hate being blindsided. But your reasoning is sound. Jason, you will need a partner. Someone that will help you out and cover your back. I was going to assign another agent, but to help keep The Library's peace I agree to assign you Mortyiene."

Jason fiddled with his satchel and glanced at Mortyiene. "Don't we have a say in the matter?" he asked, looking to give her a way out of the assignment. "Shouldn't I have a partner that has more experience with case work?"

"Under normal circumstances I would say yes. These are not normal circumstances. One, possibly two, murders have happened in relation to The Library. I have no necromancy agents. The others have full case loads, and you were there for the first murder. Bli thinkx that Mortyiene will represent the interests of the necromancers and ensure Rhyann's rights are upheld. I am willing to indulge him. If the murders are not solved then we can readdress the situation, but for now, you and Mortyiene are assigned lead investigators on this case. I am sure you will do a fabulous job, once you get used to each other."

"Lucero's family," Mortyiene said. "He must guard me. What will happen to his family if I fail to return?"

"You have been assigned to The Library Bureau of Investigation," Bli answered. "The governing bodies of all countries have agreed that The Library takes precedence over any duties requested by its citizens. My signature will keep his family safe, for the time being."

Jason's heart fluttered under Mortyiene's gaze. He couldn't believe it. He had been drawn to her from the first day he saw her at The Mountain. Now at The Library they would be working together. Jason rubbed his palms on his robes. How had they gotten so sweaty? He swallowed watching Mortyiene nod her agreement with Bli.

Bli turned his penetrating gaze back to Jason. "I will withdraw my objection to this investigator, since you have agreed to Mortyiene being his partner."

Jason rubbed his arms his skin crawling from Bli's dark gaze. He struggled to meet the liche's eyes and failed. The years of unlife had made it impossible for Jason to meet those flame eyes.

Laurel took off her glasses and rubbed the bridge of her nose. "Bli you have your agent. Mortyiene, I am sorry to put you in this position. Under normal circumstances you would have been consulted. I have read part of Jason's file when he applied to the school. I know that he has experience in solving crimes in Pegasus Cove. I do not know much about you, but if Bli thinks you are capable then so do I. Perhaps, between the two of them, they will find their answers."

"You will need these," Laurel continued, handing them each a white-gold bracelet. "Wear these around your left wrist. Once you put them on, they can only be removed by myself or the head of the LBI. They are needed to have access to sections of The Library normally off limits."

The white gold bracelet snapped around Jason's wrist. The sound caused his heart to leap. It hung around his wrist a mystical shackle that changed his life forever.

Laurel picked up a file and handed it to Jason. "Here is the case file, both bodies are currently at the morgue. Keep me apprised of your progress daily." With that, she dismissed the three of them to return to the stacks and their duties.

* * *

Jason was puzzled by Mortyiene's reaction and tried to talk to her as they wound their way back to the main hall. "Why do you hate this idea?" He asked.

"Don't you get it?" Mortyiene's voice was cold. "My friend could die over this. He was tasked with bringing me back to Eversphere. This would..." Her voice cracked with concern as she trailed off.

"Why would they kill your friend?" Jason said, concerned.

"I'm not supposed to associate with you." she snapped. "This will fly into the face of what Lucero was supposed to do."

Jason stopped. "What? Why?"

Mortyiene paused. Her shoulders shook. She put her hand on a nearby table to steady herself. "We know very little about the kind of people you are in the Rivers Alliance. We are told who and what you are and what you stand for. But actually knowing someone from the Rivers Alliance would mean that we would more information about you than what the Uver allows. If I was a librarian that would be different. I would no longer be a part of Eversphere, but, instead, a part of The Library. However, since I am only an adjunct agent I am still a citizen of Eversphere."

Jason paused a moment looking at shaken necromancer. "You mean to say that they keep our subversive influence down in your region by forbidding you from knowing us?"

"Yes, it is especially dangerous for those who use magic as we are able to know what truly happens in The Rivers Alliance. I am the daughter of a prefect in the military. That means I have a higher caste than the magic users. If I were to defect, or leave Eversphere to join with The Rivers Alliance, my family would be safe. But my friends..." Her voice trailed off. She turned to look at him. Tears welled up in her eyes.

He wanted to hug her to comfort her. He put a hand on her shoulder. She wrenched away from him. "Perhaps they will assign me someone else."

She wiped her eyes with a black linen handkerchief and looked at him. "No, it is my duty to ensure that Rhyann is not unfairly accused of the murders. Though how anyone could think she is able to manipulate the scorpions of the desert is beyond me? I must serve my home, and this is where my duty lies."

"What if Rhyann is in fact guilty of killing the Pegasus Cove soldiers?" Jason asked, curious about what the vampires fate would be.

"It is obvious you are not familiar with how vampires do battle. If she was to kill Pegasus Cove soldiers she would do it in one night and be away. No. The description of the murders sounds like something else." She plucked the file from Jason's hands. "However, if she is guilty of destroying The Library's peace we must know about it."

"What if you were assigned permanently here and Bli and the second administrator, whoever he is, signs off on it. Would that be so terrible?"

Mortyiene paused and looked at Jason. Her voice barely above a whisper so soft he had to strain to hear what she said. "No it wouldn't"

She skimmed the file as the two of them continued on their way. "I just worry that Lucero, will be held accountable and for it with his life. If it was guaranteed he would be safe, I would stay."

Chapter 4

The healer's section had a crisp, almost sterile feel to it. The books were clean. Even the spiders seemed to be hidden. The Library cats regarded Jason and Mortyiene silently. A few students and librarians started at Mortyiene's black robes. However, simply showing the white gold bracelet and Jason's own brown robes were enough to keep things quiet.

The morgue was in the back of the healer's section where they learned there was a private lift that would take them directly to the LBI floor. The medical examiner looked up when they came in. She was a striking woman with strawberry blonde hair in a high bun pulled back tight, she wore gleaming white robes trimmed with red, identifying her as a diagnostician not a caregiver. The Morgue itself was sparkling clean, not even a cat present.

"We need a report on the death of the guard."

"Ah yes, Laurel was saying you would be investigating this. I am Diagnostician Marele Dunn, Diagnostician Dunn for you two. Unlike the other disciplines, the healers use their titles even when they are librarians."

She headed toward a steel drawn about three feet wide and pulled on it. Jason noted the symbol of Levet carved into the front of the drawer. It was the same for all of them.

"Why are there carvings of Levet on all these drawers?" he asked.

The diagnostician shrugged. "Vampire kills or suspicions of vampire kills are kept in them, in case they rise." She glared at Mortyiene. "So you are the new agent that is not a Librarian. Bli must be happy to see that."

Mortyiene met her glare evenly and drew herself up to her full height. "For this case. I will need to question him." She motioned to Yule's supine form. A clean white sheet covered him.

Marele moved the sheet back from his face. The incisions were noticeable, not having been sewn up that neatly. Mortyiene ran her hands over his body, her eyes closed. "It is possible to raise him. His brain and brain stem were not disturbed." She glared at the Diagnostician, "Next time wait until I have finished with the dead before you butcher them. It is much harder, if I have to follow up after you are done with them."

"It is not our practice to let your kind near the dead after they have been sent to us."

"If I stay on, that will change. Now, I need to do my job, You may watch or you may leave," Mortyiene growled. "But either way I need to get on with it."

Jason gaped at her, stunned. His heart pounded in his chest as he heard the necromancer speak with such authority. He blinked a couple of times as the diagnostician opened, then snapped her mouth shut.

"Unseemly," she hissed at Mortyiene, "Rest assured I will let Laurel know what you have done."

"As will I. I was assigned to this case because of the need for one of my talents. You may stay or leave whichever is more comfortable for you, but the time for investigation is now. The longer he is dead the harder it is for him to remember."

The diagnostician swept out of the room slamming the door behind her. The instruments rattled in steel bowls.

Mortyiene trailed her fingers down his body. "I can raise them even if the brainstem has been severed, but they would not be able to answer any questions. If we want to find out what happened we must have the brain intact. Are you guys always so brutal with the dead?"

"Well generally no, but then again we know how they died. We are not used to talking to dead people. If the attack is a known vampire kill we burn them quickly or else we bury them."

Mortyiene nodded and took a jar out of her satchel. She dipped her finger into a clear ointment that smelled of desert sage and hawthorn. She traced a rune on the corpses forehead with the moistened digit anointing the corpse. "What was his name?" she asked Jason.

"Yule," he replied, "Yule Nodger."

"Riazfes Yule Nodger, zazsherzes f'shazhoshaz." She whispered in soft sounds. The sound hissed gently through the air promising dark returns.

Jason was stunned by the beauty of the language. Black power flared up around her and flowed over Yule. He saw a finger twitch then a hand. Finally Yule sat up and looked around with milk-white eyes. The sheet falling off his chest and pooled on his lap.

"Where am I?" he asked.

Mortyiene reached into her bag. She took out a small silver knife and cut her thumb. A drop of blood welled up, and the dead man eyed it. She dripped the blood in his mouth he grabbed her hand and suckled on her thumb like a baby would on his mother's breast. She let him for a couple of swallows, then wrenched her hand away.

"Yule," she said stroking his hair like he was a small child. "You have recently died, Do you remember?"

Yule's eyes narrowed. He shook his head. "I feel so alive." He reached for his chest as if looking for something. He ran his fingers over the incision marks and stopped. "What happened to me?"

"I need you to go back. Back to the last thing you remember." Mortyiene said.

"I remember I was at Sky Village Inn. There was a visiting bard from Lorgian. He had come in on the last caravan. The one that was attacked by the scorpions" Yule grew more animated as he told the story. "I was dancing with Cathy. She had just agreed to join with me, but it was late and I had first shift the next day."

As the man retold the story of his last night his voice grew more confident, clearer. "So I walked her home and headed back to the caravan company. I was passing by Beggars Alley when she jumped me."

"Who?" Mortyiene said, "Who jumped you?"

"A vampiress. She was tall with long brown wavy hair, it was Rhyann."

Yule got up and the sheet pooled at his feet. He was unaware that he was naked. He threw the tray with instruments across the room and dived behind another table.

"She was so strong. I couldn't stop her. She beckoned me into the alley. I had no choice. I went to her." His hand flew to his waist, trying to draw his axe that was not there. "She attacks me!" He screamed, "Stay away! leave me alone!"

He started running around the room throwing surgical instruments and trays. "No no no," Yule cried out. "Stop it!" He shrieked and collapsed twitching. The wound in his neck somehow burst open again. He had a seizure his hands knocking into the tiles, and his heels tapping out a staccato on the cold floor.

The color drained out of Mortyiene's face. As she raced next to him and, with a touch, said. *"Sheenshzes Yule."*

"What was that?" Jason said, as Yule's eyes closed and he stopped twitching.

"I've never seen anything like this. Though I have heard of it. The dead, at the level he was raised at, are truthful. They are incapable of lying. However, if what they witnessed at death was not the truth, their body's cannot handle the deception. His death was not what it appeared to be, even to him. I cannot say for certain that Rhyann is responsible, though obviously someone wants us to think she is."

Jason motioned for Mortyiene to get Yule's feet. "He did identify her. Based on this I believe we have enough to at least question her."

Marele returned to the room. She gasped as she saw all of the trays and the disarray. A pool of fresh blood was near the corpse.

"It bled," Jason said pointing to the pool of blood. Why does he smell like rotting eggs?"

Mortyiene pinched the bridge of her nose. "I knew this was going to be more complicated than I had thought." She turned to the diagnostician. "I need you to run a test for the Anacolang enzyme. While you are it, test this yellow residue." Mortyiene motioned to the yellow powder that seemed to dust the corpse. "I have reason to believe this is not a vampire kill, but another kind of death that was made to look like one."

The diagnostician look at Jason, "what happened?"

"Well, I am no expert on this kind of magic, but it appears that he thinks he was killed by a vampire. The problem is he is not acting like he was killed by a vampire." Jason replied.

"The presence or lack thereof of Anacolang will verify whether or not this is a vampire death. It is obvious he died of exsanguination but whether a vampire drained him, or something else is yet to be determined." Mortyiene explained.

Merele grabbed a couple of test tubes and gathered a sample of his blood along with the yellow powder. "Do you need to see the other body?"

Jason shook his head. "Not right now. I know how Shang died. I saw the scorpion sting. I will be going to the hive masters lab shortly to see what they can tell me of the scorpions. By the way Diagnostician, do you have a remedy for cat allergies? I have not been able to stop sneezing since I entered this damn building. Edwardynah does not seem to care that I am allergic to her."

Marele unlocked a cabinet and handed Jason a bottle of compressed tablets. "Two of these every four hours for symptoms. Here is a longer-acting one that will make you sleepy for night time."

"Are you serious?" Mortyiene asked, as they left the morgue. "You are allergic to cats?

"Yes," he said, dry swallowing a tablet. "Ever since I was a baby. Now I am here and will be for the rest of my life."

The lift to the hive masters section at the top of the administration floor rose up smoothly, propelled by thousands of enchantments.

* * *

As they rode the lift, Jason paused it for a moment. "How can you be so cold about what happened? It looked to me like Yule was in serious distress."

Mortyiene glared at Jason. "It would have been easier if your pathologist had not butchered him."

"What do you mean?" Jason turned to her.

"It has been my experience that the dead respond better to questioning if their guts have not been ripped out. For all I know, his distress was from that instead of being deceived."

"Do you not have any data on this?" Jason asked.

"It is very old, coming from centuries before. We do not cut our dead open to find answers, only to confirm answers." She paused restarting the lift. "We are gentler in our explorations than you are."

The lift door slid open at the highest floor of the administration section, the hive masters section. Jason paused, observing several spiders the size of cats skittering around. Large webs covered the walls and ceiling with several scroll shrews entangled within them.

Mortyiene chuckled. "At least you won't sneeze here," she whispered.

A hive master librarian greeted them. He wore rust-colored robes with chocolate over-robes over them indicating his station.

Jason and Mortyiene showed him their bracelets and he nodded. "My name is Baret. Let me take you to the lab."

"Thank you," Jason said. As they walked along he noticed spiders hanging in their webs and skittering along the floor. "Where are the cats?"

The librarian turned and grinned. "We are hive masters We are more comfortable with insects and arachnids. Therefore we have spiders." He pointed to a spider that was following them a short distance away. It was as big as a medium sized dog. "This is Beth she is quite friendly, though very venomous. Our spiders live as long or longer than your cats."

"I should bring Edwardynah here. Maybe she will provide a nice meal for Beth."

"I wouldn't feed your cat to her. Though your cat can come here with you and be safe. She is your guide."

He pulled up to a set of double doors. "Ah, here we are. This is the lab."

Baret opened the door to admit Mortyiene and Jason. On the tables were aquariums in which there were several species of insects and spiders. A slab at the back of the room had the dissected remains of the scorpion Jason brought with him from the desert. Standing over the corpse was the rust and brown robed hive master.

"Ah. Laurel told me you were on your way up. Welcome. I am Keikanne, the senior researcher here." She had bright yellow eyes and white blonde hair with pale skin. Blue viens wound their way up her limbs and along her cheeks.

She held out a hand, which was covered with a white cotton glove. As he shook it and he felt every frail bone in her hand. He knew, with very little pressure, that he could break every one of them. She was thin to the point of emaciation and she looked at them with her alien eyes.

"Where are you from?" Jason gasped as he shook her hand.

She smiled at him. "Do not think that all in this section of The Library come from you plain of existence. I am from somewhere else and was drawn to The Library same as you."

"What can you tell me about this scorpion?" Mortyiene said looking over the dissected arachnid.

"This is not a normal scorpion," Keikanne said. She lifed its head. "Do you see in the mandibles?"

"They look like fangs."

She nodded to Jason. "Look here." She pointed to the top of the head behind the antenna.

"Those look like horns," Jason said.

"This is no desert scorpion. Though I have no doubt it started out as one. It looks like someone or something has mutated it."

"Would that cause it to venture from its normal hunting region?"

"Desert scorpions are very territorial. They never come together except to mate, and usually the female devours the male during that interaction. To have so many of them attack your party... You were right. This was not natural. Something drove them to do this." She sighed. "I wish you had been able to get me more samples than just this one."

"Well we were somewhat limited. It took me quite a bit to convince the caravan master to allow us to bring this one in. The water reserves had been depleted by a spell. The captain was worried that the animals would not make it to the school."

Keikanne pursed her lips They formed a thin white line. "I suppose that it couldn't be helped."

"Do you think this has something to do with the nature of the desert?" Jason asked.

Keikanne looked up sharply. "What about the nature of the desert?"

"Well, these scorpions were not the only thing different. There was a sandstorm that my sorcerer friend said was not normal. The wells were not giving up their water easily. The desert nomads are restless. I have had multiple reports that the desert fells wrong."

"Tell me more," Keikanne said taking out a sheet of paper.

Jason spent the next fifteen minutes telling her about his journey across the desert.

"This is most disturbing. Yes I believe that what is happening is a result of some disturbance. By the sound of it the disturbance had been building for awhile. I will need to go out and find these scorpions and maybe their nest. Perhaps I will find answers there. Thank you for your assistance."

Jason and Mortyiene left the lab. They took the enchanted lift to the peacekeepers floor. "We should tell the peacekeepers about what Keikanne said about the scorpions. Something is actively working in the desert and they should know about it," Jason said.

"LaFlora," Jason called spotting the captain in the common area.

"Jason," she said warmly, shaking his hand.

"We are investigating the deaths of Yule and Shang. I saw you arguing with them. What were you arguing about?" Jason asked taking out his notebook.

LaFlora looked at him steadily. "Mostly about duty rosters, and what-not."

"But I heard distinctly Shang tell you that she was there and she saw what happened. What was that about?"

LaFlora looked him in the eye and crossed her arms. "Shang was trying to get out of trouble and conjured up some witness that claims to back him up. He was caught sleeping on the job. He tried to convince me it was a sleep spell and that another soldier saw it."

Jason made a note in his book. "Do you know why the desert is acting the way it is? Why it is sending up dust storms and why the wells are drying up?"

"I couldn't say. Do you think that has something to do with the scorpion attack?"

"I believe so, thank you for your time, Captain. I wanted to report that the scorpion looks like it has been intentionally mutated. The head of the hive master lab said that scorpions do not travel in packs. That the only time they come together is for mating which is usually fatal to the male. Let the militia of Sky Village know as well as the peacekeepers what we have learned. We need to take this nomad threat seriously."

LaFlora nodded and saluted, stalking off deeper into the peacekeepers offices.

"That was odd," Jason said. "What is she doing here? I thought she was employed by Red Rock Caravan Company."

"And why would she lie to us about what they were arguing about?" Mortyiene added.

"You caught that too. Well come on Mortyiene. I want to make sure that Sky Village militia knows about the scorpion attack."

They climbed the stairs to the main entry hall and headed out the door. Jason had forgotten how bright it was outside of The Library. He covered his eyes with his hand.

Mortyiene had flipped up her hood, and a sheer veil tumbled down over her face.

"Do you think skin this white comes from being out in the sun?" she asked when Jason looked at her startled.

"Aren't you hot?"

"Not really. My clothing is woven in a very breathable fabric."

Red dust clung to the bottom of her black robes and his blue and brown robes. They headed to the militia headquarters. A soldier leapt to attention and snapped a salute as Jason approached.

"We need to speak with the watch commander," Jason said, showing his bracelet.

"Right away librarian, I mean Investigator." The man opened the door and ushered them into the dim interior of the headquarters. The stone floor was spelled to keep the air a comfortable temperature. Mortyiene pushed back her hood and veil and peered around the interior.

The building was clean and free from clutter the faint smell of cleaning products tickled Jason's nose. The duty sergeant at the desk shifted nervously as they waited for the watch commander. He soon came into the main sitting area. "Investigator, Agent." He said shaking hands with Jason and Mortyiene. "What brings you out to our offices?"

"We came with a report. It appears that the scorpions that attacked the last caravan were not natural. Plus we intercepted a message from the nomads stating they were about to raid The Great Oasis. We believe that Sky Village will be attacked soon."

"I got a copy of that letter and heard about the scorpions. LaFlora was in here yesterday filing a report. I also heard from the scouts that the nomads have indeed met at Sadiq Oasis. So the hive masters think something intentionally mutated and riled up the scorpions."

Jason nodded. "I thought I would bring you the hive masters report myself." He took out the sheaf of papers that Keikanne had given him before he left.

The watch commander took them from Jason and scanned them over. "I heard LaFlora said you used to be a detective for Pegasus Cove constabulary?"

Jason shrugged. "I was. If there is anything that the watch of Sky Village needs, please come and seek me out. I will try to help if I am able to."

Mortyiene looked at Jason. "I didn't know you were a detective before becoming an investigator."

Jason turned to her. "My dad was a merchant wizard he sold his services to ships and caravans. I enjoyed figuring out puzzles and the constabulary seemed like the place to go. Puzzles and books that is. I loved it there and solved several murders, but it always felt to me more like training than actual work. I guess I was right. The Library picked me to be The Investigator."

"You got some big shoes to fill my friend, the last investigator was legendary," the commander said

"I don't intend to try to fill them. I just intend to do my job and figure out what is going on and why. I hope I will have time for my independent research while I am here."

"That you will have time for. It is pretty peaceful here for the most part. When you are needed, it will be big. Consider the watch at your disposal. My name is Samin. Welcome to The Great Oasis."

* * *

The siren sounded from over Sky Village jolting Jason from his sleep. He ran to the one window, in his office. He saw, outside, torches surrounding the great wall that separated the village from the desert.

He threw on his robes and ran to the lift that would take him to the administration floor. In the great hall the peacekeepers were organizing themselves into squads to reinforce the watch. Several Librarians, including Bli, were in the staging area awaiting assignments from incident commander Rayi.

Bli stood off to one side, surrounded by a troop of skeletons.

"We will help!" he hissed at Rayi, the peacekeeper commander.

"The men won't fight alongside the dead. Have them reinforce The Library in case the nomads break through the lines."

Bli stood still, his voice still hissing. "We can do more. fewer people will die if you let us help."

Jason strode toward the heated conversation. "Release the skeletons in the fields. There are only hedges. It will not be long before the nomads attempt to break through the hedges if they haven't already. We will be able to conserve the human forces for the main battle. The fields are too vast for us to defend them with the limited resources at our disposal."

Rayi pursed his lips into a thin line of frustration and ran a hand through curly brown hair. "Good idea librarian. Bli take your skeletons to the fields. I will have the beast masters call in the herds to the inner pens. Go now be quick." Rayi wrote out his instructions and handed a note to a peacekeeper. "Give this to Aharon let him know that the skeletons will be loosed in the fields." The peacekeeper gave a salute and trotted off in the direction of the animal pens.

Mortyiene came into the hall dressed in thigh length robes with britches and a wide black leather belt covered her abdomen. She stood next to Jason.

"Librarian, you can reinforce the front line. Agent," he said to Mortyiene, "please assist Bli in the fields."

Jason nodded and glanced at Mortyiene who sprinted toward the fields. He saw Rhyann waiting by the stairs for Mortyiene and the two of them glided out the back door.

"That's going to be trouble," he murmured to Rayi as he turned and headed out into the village.

At the wall he approached Samin. "Where do you want me?"

Samin motioned to the area of the heaviest fighting. Nomads were pushing toward the gate and scaling the twenty foot walls "Can you help out with that?"

Jason nodded, already Scarlet was on the wall lobbing out fireballs. Jason joined her. Adelaydah was further down the wall summoning illusions designed to distract the masses.

"Sizobacc." Scarlet yelled and a ball of fire streaked from her spread hands and broke over the roiling mass of mounted nomads. A hail of arrows flew toward the wall and the defenders ducked behind the crenellation.

"Loghenillun lomllhau!" Jason called. The sky lit up with forks of lightening. It struck the nomads the village roof tops and the wall.

A fork of lightening stuck the wall near Jason's feet. The concussive force blew him from the wall. He sailed through the air and landed on the hard packed earth behind the wall.

"Jason!" Scarlet screamed running down from the wall to kneel next to him. "What was that?" she asked as he lay groaning on the street.

"Lightning, I just learned the word. I guess I do not know enough syntax to control it. Around him the wounded were being tended. "I'm fine, I just had my breath knocked out of me."

"I would limit your spells to light rays." She said, helping him sit up.

Jason nodded and stood. He saw a figure flit through the streets with long wavy dark hair and black necromancer robes. What is Rhyann doing here? He thought to himself as he climbed the stairs back to the wall.

The moans of more wounded echoed from one street over as the nomads crashed through the gate. Jason scampered along the wall to the main gates. *"Nolhau Jason lull lolenun ni mouen"* A shield of prismatic light covered him. Every time an arrow hit it, it would flare up as cracks of light flowed through the shield. These cracks would weaken the protection. Jason knew it would not last long.

Scarlet cast another fireball at the raiding army. Peacekeeper units moved forward to attack those that had broken through the gates.

Off in the distant fields the sounds of screams could be heard. Jason shuddered, knowing that the skeletons would disturb the nomads.

"Mouen voulhau," He shouted. A ray of light burst from his index finger and found its mark in the eyes of one of the nomad commanders. The man screamed and fell from his horse. The press of nomads trampled the fallen commander. Hooves churning up red dust that swallowed the commanders blood.

Scarlet ran to where the gate once stood and was joined by a couple of librarian sorcerers. *"Kock sovzceta sz'wakk."* The earth rumbled at their words. A great wall of stone rose from the ground where the gate once stood. It filled the opening in the wall shutting off the nomads from the village. One nomad, unable to get out of the opening, was caught by the rising stone wall and crushed. His blood flowed down the red rock of the stone wall as it crushed him.

Jason heard screams in the streets and ran from the wall. "Hold the wall," he yelled to Scarlet. "I need to find the nomads that made it into the village."

He rounded the corner and came face to face with Rhyann. Her mouth dripped with blood as she let a body slide to the ground. "Rhyann," he screamed, "we need to find the invaders." He barely spared a glance at the dead woman. The vampire gave him a smile, her mouth tinged with red She glided off into the shadows toward the sounds of battle.

Jason charged up the street, finding small skirmishes where the peacekeepers and the militia were hard at work killing the few nomad invaders. He ran to the fields along the fence. A strange mist was covering the fields. Muffled screams hung in the air. He shuddered and left. The necromancers didn't need his help

After what seemed like hours the fighting stopped. The nomads, those that still had horses, fled from the area. Those trapped inside the village were taken into custody.

Jason headed back to the main entry into The Library. He saw Bli coming in with Rhyann. He ran to the librarian. "Mortyiene," he demanded, "where is she?"

"She was injured in the fields and sent to the hospital," Bli replied. "She will be all right."

Samin burst into the entry hall and strode toward Rhyann. "I want her arrested. She was seen multiple times draining blood, not from nomads, but from villagers. She used the cover of the raid to slake her thirst and I want her brought to trial."

Bli moved to stand in front of Rhyann. "That is not possible sir. She was with me the entire time. She could not have killed the villagers."

Samin beckoned to a small man. The man licked his lips and his hands trembled. "Is that the one you saw?"

"Yes sir. I saw that one kill my wife, she did. Right in front of me."

Rhyann stood stock still as Bli pulled himself to his full height. He towered over Samin and the nervous man. I can assure you it was not Rhyann."

"How can you be sure she didn't leave your side?" Adelaydah demanded. She had come in with Samen. "Were your eyes on her all night?"

"I do not have to answer to you, student." Bli hissed pushing Rhyann behind him.

"But you do have to answer to me," Jason said. "How can you be sure she was with you the whole fight?"

"When my skeletons march I see everything that they see. I tell you truly, Rhyann did not go to the main battle."

"I saw her as well," Jason said. "Or are you dismissing my

witness account?"

"Rhyann, go to the necromancy section and stay there," Bli said.

Rhyann headed for the lifts and left the main hall. "I will keep her confined to the necromancy section for the remainder of her stay so that you may clear her or condemn her with more evidence. I will not allow her to be killed from confused witnesses, including yourself Investigator. This was a battle and we must be sure that what you saw was the truth."

Jason nodded and turned to Samin. "She will remain confined. We will examine the bodies and find out what happened. If she is responsible, I promise I will make sure she answers for her crimes."

Samin regarded Jason. "I leave her in your care, Investigator. Right now I have to see how many of us died in that raid and get the sorcerers to remove that wall where the gates used to be."

Jason hoisted his satchel. "I will help you. I want to see those bodies Rhyann is accused of draining." He followed Samin out into the village.

The Red Rock Trading Company office had been set up as an emergency hospital. Two caregivers wearing robes of white, trimmed with deep blue, bent over the wounded. A diagnostician moved from patient to patient, writing out the treatments and leaving them with the wounded for the caregivers to administer.

"Show me the dead that were killed by Rhyann." Jason demanded of Samin. Samin took him to a storage room for Red Rock trading company. "We put them in here where it is cold."

Jason knelt next to the bodies and studied them. Their necks were torn open. Blood soaked their clothing and clung to their bodies. The faint smell of rotting eggs emanated from them. Five corpses in total were displayed.

All of them were covered with blood. Why is there so much blood? Jason thought as he attempted to lift up the shirts. In total there was three women and two men, all of them villagers.

"Do the nomads normally kill the women in raids?" Jason asked Samin who stood near him.

"Not normally. They usually do other things with the women and then leave them to die."

"How long has it been since the nomads raided Sky Village?"

"Not for over a hundred years. But if, as you say, the wells are drying up, they might think they need the oasis."

"Has there been a decrease in water of the Great Oasis."

Samin shook his head. "No. All of our springs are still flowing freely. We are able to plant food and water the livestock."

Jason sat back on his heels. "I need to look at the bodies in the fields that Bli claims Rhyann killed. I need to do it tonight."

"I can't spare anyone. You will need to have a peacekeeper with you." Samen stood his knees popping.

Jason rose to his feet. "Thank you I will ask Rayi to spare someone.

He left the company office and retraced his path back to the library. He entered the great entry way and walked up to Rayi. "I need a guard."

Rayi nodded. "I can spare Rosliniah, she is a captain and very competant. Are you sure you want to do this? I cannot guarantee your safety with just one officer."

"I should be fine. The skeletons are still out there and won't attack us as long as I am there."

He studied Rosliniah. She was tall. Her dark brown hair was cut very short. Jason could see her hard whip thin body was no stranger to the exercise room for the peacekeepers. "I am Jason good to meet you. Are you ready for a bit of investigation?"

He led the way out of the back gate to the fields. The strange mist that had covered the fields was fading in the distance. He could see the shapes of skeletons patrolling the fields. The bodies were indistinct lumps that dotted the fields.

He worked his way through the lumps. Most of them had been killed by the crude weapons that the skeletons carried, but a couple of them had deep neck wounds where the flesh was torn away. The air had a sharp metallic tang to it of drying blood. Their clothing was slightly stained crimson and the wounds still oozed a bit. He noted the puncture patterns and wounds looked like what he found in the village.

After investigating the bodies of three nomads killed from exsanguination through neck wounds. He ordered the bodies from both the village and the fields be taken to the morgue for further examination.

Chapter 5

The next morning Jason was summoned to Laurel's office. "We have found three more dead with neck wounds that look like vampire bites. I need you to go and look at them."

Jason nodded, "Of course. Do you know if Mortyiene is able to join me?"

"Yes. She was released last night. Her wounds were minor in comparison to some of the others. Your friend Scarlet made a huge difference with her rock walls."

"Scarlet is very talented, but she is very flighty."

Laurel said, "I have ordered the bodies to be taken to the Morgue. I know that Diagnostician Dunn hates it when Mortyiene raises them to ask who killed them, but this time she is prepared."

Jason headed down to Mortyiene's apartment. He knocked on her door and waited for her to answer.

Mortyiene opened the door looking paler than ever. Her right shoulder was bandaged, and her right arm was in a sling. "Bli told me you were hurt last night. Are you able to help out today?"

Mortyiene nodded. "It is just a scratch. It will heal, though I will have a scar." Her shoulders tightened.

"Do not worry. We all have scars. I got lots of them from when I was younger."

"I didn't have any, well except for my thumb. Women of my caste are not allowed to engage in anything that can harm us. This is the first time anything like this has happened."

"Are you up to raising the dead? There are a couple more bodies that look like vampire kills."

Mortyiene said, "of course, let me get my bag."

Jason studied her apartment as she gathered her black satchel. Her apartments were tidy with deep crimson matching chairs and a sofa gathered around her fireplace. He leaned against the ebony door frame and waited for her to return.

Five so far had been killed by a vampire. He knew that Rhyann could do it. She had wiped an entire village in one night but why would she attack Sky Village residents so openly.

Mortyiene returned, her black leather bag slung across her body. "Come on. Let's get this done."

The lift slid silently to the morgue. The bodies that Jason had requested were lain out on the slabs. Wooden eight pointed stars, Levet's holy symbols, rested on the chests of each of the corpses. He paused for a moment and remembered they were all suspected vampire kills. The eight pointed stars were sacred to Levet, and their presence on the corpses would keep them from rising as vampires.

"Do you have the belongings of the people that were brought in last night?" he asked Diagnostician Dunn as she moved forward to greet them.

She brought out several clear bags. The clothes inside the bags were soaked with blood and Jason studied them. He then moved to the corpses and drew back the sheet. The neck wounds were crusted over and the faint smell of rotting eggs wafted from the yellow powder that dusted the bodies. Their faces were frozen in terror.

"Raise her please," he requested.

Mortyiene nodded and took out her bottle of ointment. Dabbing her finger in it and drawing a symbol on the corpses forehead. She whispered, *"Zushavdyas anz zazsherzes shazhhoshaz."*

The woman started twitching, first her finger, then her hand. She slowly sat up. She looked around puzzled. Mortyiene took out her small silver knife and cut her thumb. She presented it to the woman who took it and drank.

"Do you know what killed you?" Mortyiene asked. "Describe it for me."

"I don't know what killed me but it looked like a vampiress. A tall vampiress with wavy black hair." The woman paused and looked around. "Am I dead?"

"Yes you are. We need to find out what happened. Can you

describe it?"

"Remember what happened to Yule," Jason murmured to Mortyiene. "We don't need another encounter like that."

"She hasn't been butchered by your pathologist. I am going to let her answer the questions."

"It was dark and confusing out there. I don't remember much. She came at me from the shadows and bit me. Bit me hard. I bled all over the place. It soaked into my clothes and my hair. I could feel the bite it hurt so much. Then I fell unconscious. I do not remember anything else until you woke me up."

Mortyiene frowned. "Are you sure about the description?"

The woman cringed, looking about the morgue. Her eyes widened in terror. "She was so beautiful in the moonlight. I was thinking it is not wise to be out on this night. Then she bit me."

Mortyiene's brow furrowed at the description. She touched the woman's head and murmured, *"sheenshzes."*

The woman lay back and closed her eyes.

"Why did she not react the same way Yule did?" Jason asked.

"Well with Yule I had asked more specific questions. Since the truth was not what he remembered, he reacted to that innate lie. For this woman I left the questions open ended. She identified something that looked like Rhyann attacked her. But since I didn't ask her if it was Rhyann and she didn't volunteer the information, probably because she had never seen Rhyann, she was able to remain calm."

"We know that Rhyann was at the battle last night. Can we be sure that she didn't leave the fields to hunt among the villagers?"

"If Bli said that she did not leave the fields then she did not leave the fields," Mortyiene said.

Jason pinched the bridge of his nose. "I am sorry Mortyiene but I must arrest her. Five people have died from what appears to be vampire attacks. Not including the attacks on the fields. It would be safer for her to be in our holding cells than under Bli's supervision."

Mortyiene glared at him and turned to Diagnostian Dunn. "Send a blood sample from these victims to analyze for the anacolang enzyme, and test this yellow substance." She turned back to Jason "I will accept your premise because she needs more protection. But I am sure she has not committed these murders."

* * *

Jason, Mortyiene, Adelaydah, Scarlet and Boris gathered for the midday meal in the cafeteria. Jason was enjoying his bowl of beef barley soup when Adelaydah spoke up.

"So when are you going to arrest Rhyann? I saw the bodies last night. They were killed by vampires. Rhyann is the only vampire here."

Mortyiene bristled next to Jason, and he put a restraining hand on her arm.

"We have not yet determined that they were vampire kills. Bli swears that Rhyann did not leave the fields and was fighting next to him during the attack," Jason said

Adelaydah slammed her fist down on the table. "What more do you need?" she yelled.

Jason jumped, shocked at her outburst.

Mortyiene spoke up with ice in her voice, "Evidence for starters. We are running tests for the Anacolang enzyme. If it comes back positive then we will know it is a vampire."

"Anacolang?" Adelaydah said, slumping in her chair. "What is that?"

"Anacolang is the enzyme that vampires exude when they bite their victims. It is an anticoagulant. We have found some bodies in the fields that Rhyann identified as her kills. Nomads who broke through the hedges around the fields. We will compare the bite size and marks between the two and test for the enzyme of the other victims," Mortyiene replied.

Adelaydah opened and closed her mouth, gaping at Mortyiene. "Promise me Jason, promise me that you will seek justice for the victims."

"Adelaydah," he said stroking her arm. "I will follow the law as I always have. If Rhyann is innocent she will be set free. I cannot hold her or try her for what happened in your village. She has the right to be here, the same as you."

Adelaydah wiped an errant tear from her eye and glared at Jason. "I just..." She trailed off. She stood up suddenly, grabbing her tray, and headed for the scullery to drop it off.

Scarlet watched her friend go and whispered, "do you really think that Rhyann is innocent?"

Jason sighed and leaned back in his chair regarding his lifelong friend steadily. "I truly do not know what to believe. The victims themselves identified her but the physical evidence is not there to back it up. Even in Eversphere the testimony of the dead is not admissible."

"The victims identified Rhyann as who killed them?" Scarlet asked.

"There are problems with the identification. We need the lab results to come in and back up their statements. Until we get them, there is nothing I can do," Jason said.

They finished their meals in silence. Scarlet and Boris got done before Jason and Mortyiene.

"You know," Jason whispered, "I really would like to have a medical examiners comparison of the bite marks. We now have a few corpses that are verified vampire kills. Perhaps the bite mark differences will answer our questions."

Mortyiene nodded finishing up her meal in silence. Jason and she took their trays to the scullery. Jason thought about what had happened the previous night as he dumped the leftover food into the garbage and slid the tray with the plates into the pass through.

As Jason and Mortyiene approached the necromancy section, several skeletons tracked them. A strange red light glowed in their eyes, signifying that Bli was watching them.

"We must detain Rhyann. We have enough evidence for a warrant. She will be safer in protective custody then outside of it," Jason whispered to Mortyiene.

Mortyiene strode next to Jason. Her chin jutted out, her black eyes flashed. "I know," she snarled, "I just hate it. We do not have conclusive proof that she is responsible"

"It is as much for her protection as for public perception. I would not want a mob coming down here demanding her blood. We know she was in the battle and so does Sky Village."

"Not even Eversphere accepts the testimony of the dead," Mortyiene whispered.

Jason paused and lay a hand on Mortyiene's arm. "This is not Eversphere. This is The Library. Tell me what is going on. Why are you so resistant to detaining Rhyann? If we detain her not only will Sky Village be safe, but she will be as well."

Mortyiene was silent for a moment and turned her back to him. Her shoulders heaved and shuddered. She faced Jason. "You don't understand what Eversphere is like. We have no crime, no drugs, no excessive drinking. We are safe and orderly, even our music and our art is very stable. Out of Eversphere life is chaotic and wild. The music and the art reflect the good and bad of the world. In Eversphere it reflects the glory of order. That you could even detain a hero of our city with only the statements of the dead is unheard of. Of course Rhyann, in Eversphere, would not even be accused of those crimes. She is old, and has been a citizen for hundreds of years. How could we think she would hurt the city that protects and honors her?"

Jason chewed on his lower lip, thinking about what Mortyiene said. "Are you happy there? In Eversphere?"

Mortyiene turned to him, "This life, this library, you, the school, everything, is a dream for me. To be able to express myself freely without fear. To get drunk, to cut my hair, to wear what I want. All of this is a dream to me, and one that will wake me up soon enough as I travel back to Eversphere."

"You want to stay here? What about your family?"

"What about them? If I am ordered by The Library to stay and be your partner, then I will be able to see them. I have a way that will keep me out of Eversphere, and, hopefully, keep Lucero's family alive and safe."

The checkout desk for the necromancy section loomed in the distance. The assistants that worked the desk were skeletons performing the basic task of stamping books that students and visitors used. Mortyiene paused before it.

"Bli, we need to see you." She said to a skeleton.

"I'll be right out," the skeleton said in Bli's voice.

"What was that?" Jason whispered to Mortyiene.

"Bli can look and act through the skeletons. You see how that one has a red glow in his eyes. That is from Bli looking through it. He can put his consciousness into any skeleton he chooses."

The door to the back offices opened. Bli glided out. He seemed to float several inches above the floor. His eyes glowed with the same red flame that was in the skeletons. Again Jason saw waves of black energy flow off him, even without the benefit of the color spell.

"We need Rhyann," Mortyiene said, handing the arrest warrant to Bli.

"She's down in Root Village at the Root Cellar," Bli said, taking the paper and looking it over. "I thought you were not going to arrest her without proof."

"Several victims have bite wounds on their necks and died from exsanguination. Furthermore we need to detain her for her own protection."

"I warned her not to go. Go get her, but do not expect people to be happy about it." Bli said, He crossed his arms and stood so still Jason could not see him move.

* * *

Root Village was an old dwarven fort that had fallen, centuries ago, to the draconic armies. Massive carved stone gates guarded entrance and egress from the village. Ramshackle houses and reclaimed rooms from the dwarven city were used by the allies of the dragon. Slaves darted to and fro, running errands. Jason's fingers clenched at the sight of them, some of them he recognized from Pegasus Cove. They had been captured in a raid.

Mortyiene laid a restraining hand on his arm. "Remember the war does not exist here."

"I recognize some of them from Pegasus Cove," he whispered back."

"I know, they were captured in a raid. They are now slaves. This is why we discourage River's Alliance from visiting Root Village."

"What would happen if they ran away to Sky Village?"

"Our agreement with Sky Village is such that the militia would return them. If they fled into The Library, and were caught, they would be killed. This is why we generally keep our borders closed to light dwellers."

Jason looked behind him at the accompanying peacekeepers, Rosliniah, Chesmue and Elifelet. Their library insignias were clearly visible on their brown tabard armor.

"Do you know where she is?" Jason asked.

"She is dead, I can always find the dead. She is at Root Cellar, an inn that has specialized in housing Vampires and other undead since the fall of Barrack Torra," Mortyiene replied, walking into the dim gray of Root Village.

"Barrack Torra -- I remember that from my studies. Most of the dwarven cities fell during the dragon attacks. Barrack Torra was one of the last to remain free because of its isolation."

Mortyiene paused a moment and looked at Jason. "Isolation was not the main problem. The way to this village is hazardous. You sky dwellers have no idea how dangerous the Gloaming is. Even when dwarves controlled all of the Gloaming, some parts were wild and untamed. The area under the red rock desert has never truly been explored. Some dim elf rangers have tried over the centuries, and most of them have died. Come to think of it, I'm not all together unhappy with my new job. Keeps me from making that trip back anytime soon."

Jason chuckled, finding some humor in her dark predictions and paused at the door to Root Cellar Inn. "Why is there no color down here? It is all so gray."

"Do you know the saying, in the dark all cats are gray?"

Jason nodded, and Mortyiene continued. "Well darkness washes out color. Our eyes need light to see color. When you are in the gloaming, what little light there is falls on the parts of the eye that cannot see color. However, inside, there is often a riot of color."

Jason could see a yellow square of light coming from a window in the tavern and heard the merry sound of a fiddle playing in the back ground. Laughter spilled from the tavern out to the streets.

"Music, laughter?" he asked.

Mortyiene smirked. "Did you think we are a dour people with no room for joy or laughter in our hearts? We are human, same as you. We have children, we have families, we live, love, and laugh the same as you." She pushed open the door to Root Cellar Inn. "It is just more subdued and needs to be government approved."

He looked over his shoulder at the peace keepers. They were from The Gloaming and knew the lay of the land and the people involved. He would not have sky dwellers involved if at all possible.

The room grew silent as he and Mortyiene entered in. Great tables were crowded not only with men, but one or two dim elves. Their coal black skin had evolved to fade into the background. Only male elves were here of course, as only men are magic users that would use The Library. Their females were moved by divine magic of their alien gods.

"Mortyiene," Lucero said, weaving his way through the tables being served by buxom wenches. They looked haggard and were in varying states of undress. "You brought him here?"

"He is the Librarian Investigator. He is the one destined to bridge the gaps between the sky dwellers and the gloaming dwellers. Do not presume to judge me for following the duty of The Library. We are here to make the detention. If she is proven innocent, or, as The Library's policy dictates, not proven guilty, she will be released. I have been assigned to the case to ensure that all of the laws and rules are followed."

Lucero fidgeted, glanced over his shoulder and stepped back. Mortyiene said in a loud ringing voice that carried over the raised cries of protest from the bar's patrons, "I am Mortyiene Bakkon, daughter of Prefect Bakkon, supreme general of Uver's troops. Does any dispute my abilities or credentials to ensure that the rights of Rhyann will be closely observed, and that her detention is not based upon her actions in war, but upon evidence as of right now?"

The bar patrons turned back to their beers and spirits muttering amongst themselves.

She glanced over her shoulder and motioned for Jason and the peace keepers to follow as she threaded her way through the bar.

Rhyann was in her rooms, sitting at a desk with books spread out before her-- library books on law and defense. "And you Mortyiene, you support this farce?"

"I support the truth Rhyann. I will have it from you, and that will exonerate you. But for now you must come with me. I will ensure that you are well treated and have your coffin moved to The Library so you may rest."

Jason looked down, noting the layer of dirt at the bottom of her coffin. He motioned for Chesmue and Elifelet to carry it back to The Library.

Jason felt his skin crawl as they walked through the bar. Rosliniah had her hand on Rhyann's arm and Rhyann's hands were cuffed behind her.

The men and women of the bar watched them as they wove through the tables to the entrance.

"Hey," a drunken voice slurred over the grumbling voices. "What's she done?"

Jason caught up to Rosliniah, the captain of the peacekeepers. "Are we safe?"

Rosliniah looked at the tavern dwellers, the mood turning uglier with each passing second.

"No," she whispered back. "She is riling up the crowd."

"Mouen lilholnun," he whispered. The area broke into a riot of color. Rhyann radiated black magic.

"Mortyiene, we need to get out of here," Jason whispered. He could feel his heart thudding in his chest. He started to sweat despite the coolness of the village.

Mortyiene drew back her shoulders and called out. "Let us pass, I will ensure that her rights are protected."

Outside, the streets were deserted. All the slaves had vanished. Whispers seemed to carry on the still air of the village.

Shadows darted along alley ways and people began to fill the deserted streets. The whispers of the crowd grew to an angry buzz. Jason glanced back over his should as the mob massed behind him.

The small procession made its way down the street. From the shadows a voice called out. "She's innocent," the cry echoed and hung in the dead air.

The buzz on the street grew to a roar as they made their way through the twisting narrow labyrinth. Pale faces appeared in windows and night soil rained upon them, thrown from the windows as they walked by.

"If she is innocent she will be released" Mortyiene said, attempting to calm the growing mob.

A rotten mushroom flew from the crowd and struck Jason on the face. He brushed off the rotting fungus with a trembling hand, his heart racing in his chest. His gaze darted to the growing mob, and then to Rhyann. She glowed with an eerie black light, sending out waves of innocence and fear. It was whipping the mob into a frenzy.

"Make her stop," he whispered grabbing Mortyiene by the arm.

"I'm trying. But she is angry, and I am not able to reach her."

"Get us out of here," he snapped at Rosliniah his eyes tightening as he gazed at the growing mob.

The peacekeepers drew their weapons and moved to the mob attempting to push them away. Someone fell on Rosliniah's sword. The air grew still as the wild eyed youth glanced down at the blade piercing his chest. His mouth opened and a trickle of blood dribbled down his chin.

"How? Why?" he asked, his puzzled eyes looking at Rosliniah, and he slid off the blade.

Jason saw a shadowy figure shot with streaks of red light behind the boy, he could hear a soft maniacal laugh that flowed over the gathered mob. The mob grew quiet as the laugh faded. A sense of stillness hung in the air. Then a roar came from the throats of a hundred villagers and the crowd pressed in on the group.

"Run," bellowed Rosliniah.

Jason grabbed Mortyiene's hand and plunged away from the mob. Mortyiene was pulling on him, trying to get him to stop. Behind them Rhyann was trying to keep up as Mortyiene was dragging on Jason's hand, slowing him down. The peacekeepers surrounded them as they raced down the street.

"Lunlmoun lomllhau lelolun." He murmured a spell and a huge globe of light appeared in the sky, illuminating all of the dark corners. Rhyann shrieked in pain at the sudden appearance of the light and Jason quickly toned it down. The mob parted before them pushed aside by the moveable ball of light.

From the shadows they came, detaching from walls and passages. Not only men and women, and elves, but things that the dark hid. Wraiths, ghosts, spell bound, the descended upon the

76

small group.

Jason felt something hard fly by his shoulder and thump into Rosliniah's shield.

"They are throwing daggers," he yelled.

"Librarian, we must get you to safety," Rosliniah bellowed.

Jason saw the entrance to The Library up ahead. In the door way was the skeletal figure of Bli awaited him. A small platoon of skeletons stood outside of the great door to The Library. Another fell under the sword of the peacekeeper. A woman screamed as Chesmue and Elifelet dropped the coffin and one of Chesmue's daggers sprouted from her throat.

"Mouen voulun." Jason cried, a ray leapt from his finger and hit an ethereal being. It dissipated the form that whirled with a cold mist and vanished from sight.

"Can you keep them at bay?" he yelled to Mortyiene.

"No, the ghosts are too powerful, I have not gone through the second chamber yet."

"Then cover her." Jason yelled, "I have to slow down the crowd.

"Lunlmoun lomllhau lelolun," Jason yelled. A small sun formed in the square floating above the mob. The life giving rays of the sun reflected a hundred times over in the myriad of crystals upon the walls. Mortyiene leapt at Rhyann with her cloak covering the vampire as the false sun's rays hit her. The light poured through the streets and the dark dwelling Gloaming citizen's, screamed and fell back. The shadows of ghosts and wraiths turned from the presence of the bright light and fled away their unearthly cries echoing through the ruined halls.

"Come on. We do not have much time," Jason said, sprinting toward The Library door.

Mortyiene nodded and grabbed Rhyann's hand, covering her with dark force that reflected the sun's rays. *"Sazvias siezchzes Rhyann."*

Chesmue and Elifelet had fallen back during the mob attack

and with one final push Jason, Mortyiene and Rosliniah made it through the light addled mob. Two skeletons slammed the door shut behind Jason and the peacekeepers.

Bli stood in front of them his arms crossed. "Well that did not go well."

Jason slumped against the door that the peacekeepers were sealing shut. "A master of understatement sir. I need this prisoner taken to the peacekeepers cells, Elifelet and Chesmue are still out there. They were overcome by the mob. I would ensure she remains alive for her trial and interrogation."

Bli nodded. "I was going to request this. Where is her coffin?"

"Out there," Jason motioned to the door. "I'm sure it is ok, as they would not dare mess with her coffin. She is, after all, the vampiress Rhyann, The Butcher of Melagate."

With that, he turned to the vampire. After you have been processed in booking, I will be interrogating you. I need your side of the story, but understand this, though I find no evidence, at this time, that you have committed these murders. it does not mean that there might not be evidence down the road. Yule identified you as his killer and I have to take that into account."

With that, he turned and strode to the lift that took him back to his rooms. Mortyiene paused for a moment and murmured *"Zecheizes Rhyann,"* a spell to help heal the vampiress. She hurried after him to his office.

* * *

The interrogation room was a riot of color that represented all of the major schools. The room's white walls stood in stark contracts to the blue tiled floor. A plain brown table had red, green and black chairs pushed around it. Jason understood that the presence of all the colors was to promote neutrality. However, all it accomplished was a headache. The colors were rather odd to Jason's eyes. They seemed to clash and make the room chaotic looking. The LBI was neutral and when someone was interrogated it was important that they understand that Library Law superseded all other law.

Rhyann sat in a chair opposite Mortyiene and Jason. Jason had a notebook in front of him as well as an enchanted always full pen. Outside of The Library these pens were rare and highly sought after. In The Library they were quite common as every enchanter was expected to make several gross of them. One of the gifts The Library gave out to graduating students were these pens.

"Where were you two nights ago?" Jason started with just the perfunctory question.

"Root Cellar Inn, in my rooms, studying for classes." The vampiress responded quietly. "I had dinner earlier a lovely human male donated for me. I had no reason to murder the guard."

"How do you know we are speaking about the guard? I am fairly sure that I did not mention his death."

Power rolled off of the vampiress and she fixed his eyes in hers. "Do not take me for a fool Librarian. I know that you are here because of his death, and the deaths of the villagers last night. Yes I was at the battle, but I was with Bli in the fields, not in the village."

Jason swallowed and forced his eyes from hers glancing down at his paperwork. "Were you responsible for the deaths at Melegate? Did you recognize the guards from there?"

"Melegate?" The vampiress voice cut through his musings. "I will not answer questions relating to that city. It is out of your jurisdiction."

"I am just attempting to find out more about the victims in this case. It appears that they were also at Melegate, and I am just establishing that you were there as well."

"That was war. We all must do things during the time of war that we do not wish. Melegate, for me, was no exception. I was there, but I do not remember those guards. I did not tarry long when the soldiers came. I called a retreat and we, my minions and

I, fled. I did not see any of the soldiers."

Jason scribbled a note in his book while Mortyiene stiffened next to him. "Jason," she whispered, "we can neither detain her nor question her on those actions, or hold her accountable."

He motioned Mortyiene to follow him outside. Once they were in the hall and Jason shut the door behind them. Jason turned to her. "I know that, but, I cannot help but think that somehow what happened in Melegate is connected to the murders."

Mortyiene nodded and they both headed back into the interrogation room. "So you are unable to account for your whereabouts two nights ago." Jason said, " I find it odd, Rhyann, that soldiers from Melegate are being killed, while you are here. Are you certain that you are not finishing what you started?"

Rhyann stood up, catching his eyes in hers. "I am not responsible for their deaths." Her voice washed over him, enfolding him in black warmth. Suddenly Mortyiene touched his hand and the warm black cleared away from him. He shook himself as if waking from a dream.

"Rhyann," Mortyiene said, "If you continue this use of your powers I will arrest you and stake you myself. You know the use of your mesmerism is illegal in the confines of The Library."

"He's annoying me," Rhyann said.

The light in the interrogation room stabbed his eyes as Jason shook himself awake.

"You said you were studying that night. What were you studying?"

Rhyann frowned a moment, a crease forming between the flawless eyes. "I don't recall. That is odd, huh, I usually remember everything."

"What do you mean you don't recall?" Jason stood up and towered over the sitting Rhyann.

Rhyann met his eyes without blinking. "Just what I said. I don't remember."

"So no one can verify you were in your rooms all night,

including you." Jason demanded.

"So it seems," the vampiress said in a soft voice.

"Oluhjallhau Jason l'yloolaulaylunloo la wallenun lath mouenun," Jason whispered.

Immediately the world jumped into a panorama of colors. A deep black surrounded Rhyann. He stared at her, trying to filter out the light color.

"Mouenhau mouen" Jason spoke, making his voice clearer.

The aura around Rhyann grew brighter. The black turned to gray and a lighter shade of gray, but also purple. At first the purple was so deep that it was black, but with the additional light it grew lighter until it became a violet.

"Did you work with any illusionists?" Jason asked.

"Illusionists?" Rhyann asked in a puzzled tone.

"Yes your whole aura is tinged with purple. It looks like an illusionist cast a spell on you not long ago."

"Could the spell block my memories?"

"A powerful enough illusionist could make it seem like you did something that you did not do."

Rhyann frowned. "I don't know of any illusionists at the school. How old is the spell?"

"It is fairly recent and strong," Jason answered. He studied the vampiress who was growing more agitated as it sunk into her the implications of an illusionist setting her up.

"Rhyann," Jason said, standing suddenly, "I am going to put you in protective custody Do not leave here unless I specifically request it of you or Mortyiene. You may leave for your classes if Mortyiene and three peacekeepers are with you, but aside from that you must stay here."

With that he rose and headed out the door, Mortyiene hard on his heels.

"What is it?" she asked.

"Not sure, come on." He sprinted toward the lift that would take him directly to the healer's floor.

The lift took him straight to the medical examiners floor. He showed his bracelet along with Mortyiene and headed for the morgue.

He pulled open the draw that was holding Yule's corpse and whispered the two spells again. The aura around Yule grew lighter until it too was a deep purple that looked black. Only this time there were streaks of grayish red in the purple.

He slammed the drawer shut. "Illusions, and very good ones I believe."

"Illusions. Someone is using magic to change the signatures and throw off our investigations? That means anyone could be responsible."

"We need to access their military records. I will talk to Rosliniah tomorrow. Keep Rhyann here in the holding cell, the sentiment in Sky Village being what it is. I do not trust that she is safe even in The Library."

"Tomorrow, shouldn't we go out tonight?"

"Rosliniah is probably in bed right now, and I am exhausted. I am going to get a couple hours of shut eye. I will assign a couple extra peacekeepers to LaFlora which should help keep her safe. She knows what happened there."

Mortyiene nodded and they both walked back to the lift. At the LBI wing they assigned extra guards to keep the captain safe, and Jason made his way back to his own rooms deep in the heart of the wizardry section of The Library.

* * *

Jason tossed and turned, his legs getting tangled in his blankets as he dreamed. He was in a long hall that extended down. Along the edges of the hall were twisted medical equipment. He recognized it from the hospital section. But this was no hospital, this was something else.

He floated up through a poisonous green atmosphere and dove

through a green shimmering portal that dumped him into The Library. The stacks of books towered above him, chaotic in size and shape, and gleaming in the torchlight.

He wandered through the stacks, searching for a reason. Spiders chittered in high chaotic webs. Their sleek black bodies gleamed in the torchlight, watching him.

The sound of chanting drew him further into the stacks. Four voices droned in a strange language he did not recognize. He paused for a moment to get his bearings. The sounds of chanting echoed through the strange shaped stacks.

Bookcases were asymmetrical, built at odd angles, yet somehow keeping the books in their shelves. He started to run. He had to find the chanting that was so important.

He ran faster, the bookcases and tables flying by him. He searched for the chanting. His heart was pounding in his chest and his sides ached. His body was covered with a thin sheen of sweat as he raced along the stacks.

He burst into their circle, unable to make out any words. He pulled to a stop, watching them. Four of them stood in a circle on an etched pentagram in the floor. Jason studied the symbols. The words of the chant blurred into a cacophony of sound.

As Jason strained to hear the words, one word kept repeating itself. Shax, Shax, Shax. He studied the figures, feeling one was female and the rest were male, but darkened hoods concealed their faces and bodies so he could not be sure.

The same poisonous green portal he had flown through from the alien landscape opened in The Library. A monstrous leg, like that of a giant bird, stepped out of the shimmering portal. The chanting grew louder, more frantic, as clawed hands forced open the portal. A figure stepped out. Taller than the stacks, taller than the humans, it roared in triumph. Its form shimmered and shifted until it looked like Rhyann. Its dove like eye pierced through the darkness into Jason's heart.

With a start Jason awoke, gasping. He limbs tangled in the bed clothes. He struggled to breathe. He made his way to his kitchen and splashed some water on his face. He gulped down some water and used the counter for balance. The dream started to fade, but the sense of foreboding grew.

Chapter 6

Jason shifted uncomfortably on the hard seat in The Library's auditorium. He was stuck in a lecture about the linguistics of magical languages. He groaned, not looking forward to the class. He had to take it in order to enter the second Mana Chamber, the mystical chamber that would open his mind to more powerful spells.

Boris had folded himself in a chair too small. Jason grinned at the huge beast master, feeling sorry for him.

Jason turned his attention back to the lecture. Librarian Jodian had to be the most boring lecturer in the school. He had been an enchanter, at one time. Jodian's under robes were a dirty gray, and his outer robes were a stained brown. Greasy brown and gray locks hung down in front of tired brown eyes. His lectures were enough to cure anyone of insomnia.

"Each language," Librarian Jodian said, in a low monotone voice, "has its own unique sound. You can identify the spell casters by the sounds of the language."

Adelaydah jabbed Jason in the ribs as he drifted off. "You are snoring," she hissed.

Jason snapped awake. He turned his attention to the lecture. "I had a nightmare last night and did not sleep well." He whispered to his friend. He rubbed his eyes and yawned. "This lecture is not helping me stay awake." He stretched over the back of the chair. His back popped as he bowed over the back of the chair and he felt blood rush into tired muscles.

Librarian Jodian continued. "Spell casters are born with a grammatical predisposition to a magical language. This is in addition to everyone's innate ability for grammar of the common tongue. Some scholars theorize that spoken grammar is an instinct. They cite three year olds can speak complex sentences that they have not heard before. Vocabulary is learned, grammar is instinctual. At least grammar in the verbal form is. I have read some of your papers. I am positive that written grammar is not instinctual." He laughed dryly at his joke and nervous titters dotted the audience as people attempted to share his humor. He turned back to the lectern and shuffled his note cards.

Mortyiene was seated three rows back with her friends, Lucero and Rhyann. Jason felt her gaze on him. His heart fluttered in his chest. The pen was clutched in a sweaty palm as he bent over his notebook taking notes. He longed to turn around and look at her. Her presence was cool night compared to his bright day.

Rhyann was on temporary release from protective custody so she could attend this lecture. He glanced around at the several members of the peacekeeper's force watching both Rhyann and the students.

"So when you hear the soft rolling l's of wizardry or the hisses of the s and sh sounds of necromancy you can identify what language. There are eleven major schools," Jodian continued. "Though there is some overlap. You can easily identify the languages based upon the sounds that you hear in each of them."

"Wizardry, as I have said before, has soft rolling l sounds. Necromancy has syllabant s and sh sounds. Sorcery has hard k and q sounds. Illusionist's have h and th articulations. The three natural languages, or languages that work with living things that are not humanoid, are the languages of beasts, plants and insects. Beast masters make sounds that sound like a cat purring. Hive masters click, as if insects are chripping. Plant masters have the harder R sound in their vocabulary."

He poured himself a glass of water from the pitcher on the lectern and took a deep swallow. "There are three more languages as different from each other and night and day. The language of healers is one of g's and j's. Whereas thaumaturgy, the study and summoning of the infernal and abyssal, is hard x's. And Enchanters, when they do speak their language, is indistinguishable from wizardry."

"Understanding the syntax of the vocabulary of each school.

It will help you identify what you are working with or against. This can translate into adjusting your shield harmonics in wars. will allow you to determine what is the most effective spell. The subtle variations of tone will determine and manipulate the spells accordingly."

He paused for a moment, looking over the students. "Language in spell casting is precise. It must clearly state your intent. You will spend the rest of your life studying the linguistic and vocabulary for your language and how it impacts spells."

"Can someone learn more than one language?" Lucero asked. His dark brown eyes riveted on Librarian Jodian.

"An interesting question, and the answer is yes and no. Not even the long lived-elves. or the undead masters are able to learn two languages. It is set in them at birth. With the exception of one language-- that is the language of thaumaturgy. Scholars have pondered this phenomenon for centuries. Thaumaturgy is the language of the infernal and abyssal. That means it is the language of demons and devils. These are two different creatures with one goal, to lie. It is believed that thaumaturgy is a parasitic language. It latches onto a spell caster and whispers promises of whatever the spell caster desires most. The problem is, it lies. Your own soul is in jeopardy. This will happen even if you are dead."

"This makes thaumaturgy a very insidious discipline. When you cast a spell, its words will be woven into the syntax of other languages. Any other questions?" Jodian asked.

Everyone was silent. Adelaydah tensed beside Jason as she bent over her scroll, writing fast.

"There will be a quiz tomorrow on the languages and what they sound like, after which you will break into your independent disciplines to learn advanced techniques. When you have completed your vocabulary memorization, you will be assigned a time to visit the Mana Chamber. This will open your mind to a higher syntax. Please, do not visit the Mana Chamber until your assigned time. Students unprepared for the chamber have had aneurysms and strokes." With that final word he dismissed class, and headed back to his office.

"Interesting," Jason drummed his fingers impatiently as the students filed out of the auditorium. "I was at the crime scene where the guard's body was found. Mortyiene was there as well. We found more of that yellow residue close by."

"Yellow?" Adelaydah shoved books into her satchel. She turned to look at Jason. Her brow furrowed. "It could be sulfur. The desert is full of sulfur springs. I think it is all over the place."

"Maybe," Jason said. "You are probably right. Still, it is odd. I wonder. However, it is indisputable that he died of exsanguination. He was drained dry through two puncture wounds in his neck. Plus there have been a number of dead villagers with the same marks. Rhyann also stated she did not remember where she was, or what she was doing when Yule died."

The friends shoved their books and notebooks into their bags and hoisted them over their shoulders.

Jason sneezed a couple more times. "Damn cats," he muttered as they filed out of the auditorium. He glanced briefly at Mortyiene and Rhyann as he left the huge room.

As Jason left the room Barnabas intercepted him. "Director Laurel needs to see you and Mortyiene in her office right away."

Jason looked up and caught Mortyiene's eye. He motioned for her to come over. "What is going on?" Jason asked, adjusting the satchel on his shoulder. His sinuses congested from the cat fur. "Another murder?"

"I am not sure," Barnabas replied. "I was just told to get you."

"Why did you call me over?" Mortyiene asked, as she joined Jason and Barnabas.

"Director Laurel needs to see us." Jason felt calm. Perhaps I am getting used to this, he thought. No I cannot get used to murder. He stretched his arms toward the ceiling to get circulation going after sitting for so long.

Mortyiene's eyes widened, and she fell in step next to Jason.

They made their way to the LBI headquarters.

"Come in," Laurel called, when they knocked on the door.

Laurel's office was dominated by three desert nomads. They were clothed in reds and yellows of the Singh clan. The most elaborately clothed one sat in one of the three chairs opposite Laurel. The other two stood on either side of the door and glared at Jason as he entered.

"Jason, Mortyiene, this is Sarad, of the Singh Clan desert nomads. He has come with a request." Laurel said, introducing the man.

"Sarad," Jason cried. "You wrote that letter to Shang."

Sarad looked at Jason. "So you found it. I did write that letter. However, it has come to my attention that we of the desert must work with Sky Village and the great oasis." His harsh voice echoed years of yelling over desert winds.

Mortyiene slide into the remaining chair. She took off her own satchel and set it beside her on the floor. Behind Sarad stood the other nomads, their arms crossed as they glared at the librarians.

"I thought there had been peace here for hundreds of years. The Library had never denied you access to the springs and the fields." Jason pulled the strap of his satchel over his head, taking off the heavy bag. He dropped it to the floor, and sank into the chair.

"It is true, but a couple of years ago that changed. The waters started to retreat from the springs. The hidden springs, the ones that only we know about, also retreated. We blamed it on the villages and The Library. Now I am not so sure."

"What happened to change your mind?" Jason asked.

"The night of the raids several of my riders died from neck wounds and bled out. Your militia was kind enough to let us collect our dead. However, the next morning three women and four children were also found drained of blood. All had the same kind of bite marks. Their bodies were covered with blood and a fine dusting of yellow powder. We heard about the attacks on your militia. We believe they are related."

"So you want us to go with you to your camp and look at them?" Jason asked, making a note in his notebook.

"If you would Investigator. We believe that we are cursed. The same curse is what is attacking members of your own village. Perhaps we could work together to discover the truth of what is going on."

Jason leaned back in his chair and looked at Mortyiene. "When would we leave?" He asked.

"We are prepared to take you to the camp this evening." Sarad replied. "It is our hope that hostilities will be buried if we can find the source of this curse together."

"As do I. I will be happy to help bury this unhappiness between our peoples." Jason stood and bowed low over his hands, mimicking Sarad's own greeting.

Sarad stood and did the same. "With your permission, Director, we would return to the inn and await the evening fall. From there we will guide the investigator and his partner to our camp."

"Of course Sarad," Laurel rose and bowed over her hands as well.

The nomads left the office. Jason remained standing, looking at the Director. "Do you think this is a plot to kidnap us?"

Laurel dropped to her seat. "Possibly, but doubtful. You are friends with Boris, the beast master student. Take him with you to calm the animals."

Jason looked at her. "I still do not like this. We will be going with no other backup than a couple of peacekeepers and our bracelets. If they are being attacked by the same thing that attacked the villagers, we should know about it. I just worry this is a trap to lure me out of the protection of the Library. After they get me to their camp they may launch another attack at the Library." He clenched his fists leaving half moon creases in his hands.

"They have offered you hospitality. This is sacred to the nomads." Laurel shook her head in sympathy. "Go and get ready.

You have a long ride ahead of you."

Jason and Mortyiene walked to the lifts. "I have never ridden a horse," Mortyiene whispered. "I have ridden tharlions but never a horse."

Jason stopped and stared at her. "Not even around Eversphere?"

"I have never left the city on an overland route." She chewed on her lower lip.

"Surely," Jason paused, "you have seen horses?" He rolled his eyes to the ceiling and sighed.

"Of course I have. I have just never ridden one. Ladies of my caste do not ride horses. It is considered..." She mused searching for the right word, "...unseemly."

"Well Boris will pick out a quiet one for you. Come on. Lets go to the peacekeepers headquarters and request Rosliniah to accompany us."

The peacekeeper's quarters were quiet. Rosliniah sat in the corner with her friends, Chesmue and Elifelet. Jason showed his bracelet to the guard and they walked over to the trio. "I see you got out of Root Village."

Chesmue grinned at him. The smile made it to his orange eyes. "It takes more than a small mob to stop us. We made it back a few hours later with Rhyann's coffin in tow."

"Captain, we need an escort." Jason requested looking at the four peacekeepers.

Rosliniah looked up. "Of course Investigator. Where to?"

"We are being taken to the nomad camp. They have had several kills in their village similar to the attacks here at The Library. They have asked that we come."

"You're going to the nomad camp?" Chesmue asked, his strange orange eyes growing rounder.

"Yes, and we need our own escort."

"I and my companions will escort you. Meet us here at sunset and we will ride in the night," Rosliniah said. She slammed her right fist into her chest and then held her hand out over the floor, a peacekeeper salute.

"Of course. My thanks Captain." Jason said, inclining his head in her direction. "Come on. We need to find Boris." Boris was out in the fields working with the cattle. His huge face broke into a great grin when Jason and Mortyiene exited The Library.

"Jason, what brings you out to the cattle pens?" Boris asked. He lumbered over to the couple, slapping his gloves on his thigh. "Something good and different, I hope."

"We are heading to the nomad camp this evening. We need your help in tending the animals. Also, Mortyiene has never ridden a horse before."

Boris looked Mortyiene up and down. "I have the perfect beast for you lady. She is gentle yet tough." The huge man turned his deep brown eyes back to Jason. "I would be honored to join you. There is a camel master in the nomad camp that I would love to talk to."

Jason smiled at his friend, finally something going right. "Well that is good news. Meet us at the main entrance to The Library at seven pm. Bring enough horses for three peacekeepers as well. The nomads have their own horses."

Boris nodded and returned to his work. Jason looked at Mortyiene. "That is settled. Now all we have to do is our own packing.

* * *

The sun had set by the time the train of horses and people wound their way out of the gates. The spring night air was fragrant with the desert honeysuckle. Off in the distance heavy clouds fought their way over the mountains.

Sarad and his two clansmen pointed their horses to the West and headed toward where the sun had set.

Above, the stars stood out in stark contrast to the night sky. A panorama of twinkling white lights included the great ghost trail down the center of the stars.

Mortyiene clutched the saddle pommel with both hands as the placid palomino mare followed Boris's huge bay gelding. Jason rode a slender chestnut mare that champed at the bit, eager to be going. The nomads had their own slender horses, and the desert was peaceful as they rode to the camp.

The Library dwindled a small speck on the horizon. As the sun rose in the eastern sky, the group saw the campfires in the distance. The nomads, eager to get home, sped up the gate of the horses.

"Come on," Sarad said. "They will have hot food and beverage waiting for us." He urged his horse into a trot. The other horses sped up to join it.

Jason looked over at Mortyiene who was clutching her saddle. Her reins dangled from her hands as she bounced up and down in the saddle. Her feet pointed out in odd angles. He rode up next to her to calm her down.

"Is..it..always..like..this?" Mortyiene gasped as she clutched the pommel, her face even whiter than normal.

Jason grinned and shook his head. "We will be there soon."

Women were crouched over campfires. The scent of breakfast greeted them. Jason smelled the scent of coffee brewing. His stomach rumbled despite his nerves. Meat heavily spiced and sweetened with honey filled the camp with enticing aromas. Two tribesmen rushed up to tend their horses. Jason swung down from his saddle. He motioned that Rosliniah, Chesmue and Elifelet should allow Boris to tend their horses.

"Come friends, let me welcome you to my home. You will stay with me and as long as you are a guest you shall be safe," Sarad said.

Jason surveyed the camp looking for signs of hostility. Around him nomads were eyeing him. He pulled his satchel over his shoulder. As he scanned for threats he noticed the single nomad women looking at him with frank eyes. His stomach twisted in knots as he turned his attention back to Sarad.

Jason noticed his blisters, that were nearly healed, had burst open again. He groaned and rubbed the insides of his thighs. Mortyiene walked a strange bow legged style. The insides of her thighs were obviously bothering her.

Jason followed Sarad into a huge yurt twice as big as the yurts the caravan used. The floor was covered with brightly woven rugs and radiated cool from the ground beneath. Sarad lay back on cushions that were strewn around, while his wife prepared food and coffee for him and the guests.

"Let's refresh ourselves before we attend to the dead. We have laid them in the preparation hut, waiting to be burned. We held off cremating them in hopes that you would make haste and come quickly."

Jason nodded his thanks. He motioned for his companions to be seated. All had filed in, save for Boris who was off looking at the camels and speaking to the camel master about their care.

Jason's eyes watered at the taste of the spicy food. He gulped down cold water. Curry and other spices burned his tongue and the sensations spread as he drank. Mortyiene chuckled at his reaction and ate more slowly, drinking chilled mint tea.

"When did your men and women start dying?" Jason asked as he ate his food. He wiped his eyes with his handkerchief.

"Two, no three nights ago we saw the first strange death. Though the numbers of the dead have been growing." Sarad ate and drank his own coffee and food.

Bilee, the wife of Sarad, spoke up as she served them. "Two more and another child were killed last night while you were away, my husband."

"Truly?" Sarad sat up straighter his eyes subdued and dark.

"Yes, my husband. Mikah and her husband, along with their daughter Diayah, were killed." Bilee's voice cracked from sorrow. Her own dark brown eyes down cast. She was unable to meet her husbands eyes.

"I will speak with the families about this." His eyes grew

94

troubled. "I do not know what to do about this plague. It seems to destroy,but for no reason."

They finished eating their meal in silence. "Bilee, I am going to take our guests to the tent of preparation. After the investigator examines the dead we will allow them to kiss the fire." Sarad turned to Mortyiene. "Know this necromancer, you may not raise them. It is considered unclean by our kind. We cannot allow you to desecrate their remains."

"Of course Sarad," She replied, the tension flowed out of her body. Her breath coming out in a soft rush "I shall honor your traditions."

Jason dropped back next to Mortyiene as they followed Sarad to the tent of preparation. "Are you all right? I have never seen you balk at raising the dead?" He whispered, as his feet shuffled through the red dust and dirt.

"I think we can get all of the answers we need without raising them. The day is hot. There will be flies and smells. I would rather not deal with them."

Jason frowned, but accepted her explanation. The tent of preparation was on the far outskirts of the camp, away from the water and most of the people. The bodies were laid on rush mats. Each bore a carved lightning bolt, the holy symbol of the god Ishkataar on their chest.

"I did not know the nomads followed Ishkataar." Jason studied the symbols on the covered bodies.

"The great lord of the sky is always over us so we honor him," Sarad said.

Jason knelt next to a corpse and pulled back the sheet. It was one of the first corpse's and was dressed in fresh clothing. He touched the bite mark on the corpses neck and took out a tape to measure it. He made a note in his notebook about the depth and size. "You prepared this one? I thought that you did not prepare them." Jason noted to Sarad.

"This man died the first night. It happened before we realized that something was stalking us. It is our tradition to prepare and burn the dead right away. So we did. The ones that died later were not prepared."

Jason spent an hour pulling back sheets making sketches and taking measurements. "These were all killed by the same thing. Notice how the bite marks are the same size. See the imperfection in the teeth right here." He pointed to a crooked bite mark. "These all look like the same thing that attacked Yule and the villagers."

He covered the bloody corpses back up. " Do you have anyone that died from the attack on the Oasis that was bit by the vampire there?"

"One. He is over here. We have not prepared him for the fire kiss."

Jason gently pulled back the sheet and studied the bite marks. They were identical. The hot desert air had dried the sweat stained body. The wounds were crusty. Jason smelled the coppery smell of dried blood. The air in the tent smelled like rotting eggs. Jason made several drawings and impressions of the bite marks and looked at Mortyiene. "These bite marks are identical to the others. Somehow I think I am missing something."

Mortyiene bent over the man and looked at his wounds. "This feels like a vampire attack but the others..." She trailed off, uncertain about what to say.

"Thank you Sarad. We have the information we need. You are now free to dispose of your dead in the way you wish."

They followed Sarad back to his tent while men entered into the tent of preparation. They watched as the nomads took the bodies to a pyre that had been built from horse dung and palm fronds.

"Rest here my friends. You are not allowed to see the kiss of fire. It is our most sacred rite. We appreciate that you have come but I must insist you stay here." Sarad crossed his arms.

Jason nodded, exhausted by the ride. He and his companions collapsed on the cushions drained of energy. Jason could hear the chanting of the tribesmen as they burned the bodies scattering, the ashes into the winds. He fell into a restless, fitful sleep.

* * *

The journey back was uneventful. Jason tumbled into his bed for a few hours of sleep. He kept dreaming about the bodies and the bite marks over and over again. He tossed and turned, sure he was missing something important.

The next day he was busy with classes. He did not have time to worry about the case until after he finished his last class.

Scarlet and Adelaydah walked up to Jason arm in arm. He glanced up from his conversation with Mortyiene as the girls approached.

"We're heading to Sky Village Inn for dinner and some dancing. I hear there is a great bard there. We need to blow off some steam. Do you want to come?" Scarlet said. Her green eyes danced with anticipation.

Jason looked at Mortyiene and smiled. "Sure. Let me drop off my books. You want to join us?"

Mortyiene nodded. "Sure, that sounds like fun. I need to let Lucero know I won't be joining him. He worries about me. He won't come to Sky Village." She fingered her white gold bracelet absently.

"Great, we will meet up in the entry hall in a half hour," Scarlet said.

Jason went back to his rooms and changed into his silk sky blue robe. He grabbed his embroidered brown over-robes. He ran his fingers through his hair. Cupping his hand over his mouth and nose, he checked his breath. Grimacing a bit he brushed his teeth.

Shouldering his satchel, he headed down to the waiting area where Scarlet, Boris and Adelaydah were waiting for him. As he got there he spotted Mortyiene coming out of the lift from the Draconic section of The Library.

Adelaydah regarded her with a cool look. "Nice to see you again," she said, extending her hand.

Boris caught Mortyiene up in a big hug. Mortyiene's face screwed up from the smell. He had spent the day tending to the herd animals outside and learning about veterinarian medicine. Though his hair was set from a shower, he still smelled of animals.

"You must take me to see the Tharlions soon," Boris said. "I have always wanted to speak to them and find out more about them."

Mortyiene pushed him away. "Of course I'll make arrangements. I am sure I can get you into the pens."

Laughing, the friends went out into the night, heading toward the Sky Village Inn. Jason and Mortyiene paused. Mortyiene looked up at the night sky. The moon hung low over the western horizon. Its waning light brightening the village streets. Her face unreadable Jason paused for a moment and followed her gaze.

"I miss the stars," she murmured.

"Of course, most of your work is done at night, but here you are not able to go outside often." Jason slipped an arm about her waist.

Mortyiene followed him to the tavern. "The best part of our trip was riding under the stars."

The light and sounds coming from the tavern filled the night air. The merry scrape of the fiddle and a clear tenor drew them to Sky Village Inn. This was an outstanding bard.

A bard could bolster up or break down defenses. Armies used them to bring terror to their enemies. However, Jason had learned, that most bards were content making other people happy. They seldom went into deeper mysteries.

Inside, Boris and Scarlet were already whirling around the dance floor. Her hair sent out little sparks of flame as she danced. Her red robes, specially designed for dancing, floated about her like living flame. The harmless flames, that whirled about her, were from a simple vanity spell.

Adelaydah and a young man, Jason did not know, were also dancing. A panorama of stars floated from her purple robes. She wove illusions with the music. It looked like stars were dancing with her. The young man's lithe body spun her about. His feet picking up the rhythm that matched the twinkling of the stars.

Jason scanned the room and pulled Mortyiene over to the empty table in back, where the others had left their bags and wraps. It was hot in the tavern, having been warmed by the sun. Even the cooling night didn't decrease the heat much. He had forgotten how hot it was outside The Library.

A waitress wove through the crowd, laden with food and drink orders for his friends.

"I'm Kailah. What would you like tonight?" She was a plump woman with a freckled bosom. Red curls enhanced the smattering of freckles across her perky nose.

"What's on the menu?" he asked, slipping the satchel from his shoulder.

"A fresh beef joint on the fire, and chicken stew. We also have pork roast with potatoes. And mushroom soup made of Gloaming truffles and buttons."

"Gloaming mushrooms?" Jason was awed. He had never had anything made with Gloaming mushrooms. Trade between Draconic and River's alliances were strictly banned.

"Aye. This is part of library land. We do trade with the people from the Gloaming here," Kailah replied.

"I'll have some of that joint, a bowl of soup, and some bread." Jason said.

"I'll have chicken stew and some bread," Mortyiene said, "I grow weary of mushrooms. They were the main staple of our trip. The caravan had specific plots it would tend."

His friends returned and slid behind their plates. The illusions and the fire died down as they sat.

"What took you so long," Adelaydah said, eating her dinner.

"We stopped to look at the stars." Jason patted Mortyiene on her arm. "She does not get to see them that often. Last night she was concentrating on the horse and did not have time to look at them."

"Are you still investigating Shang and Yule's deaths?" Scarlet asked, taking a sip of mushroom soup and rolling her eyes heavenward.

Jason nodded. "We are not sure Rhyann did it. We have our suspicions, but no real proof. Until we get proof we will detain her except for her classes. She will have a guard with her when she does go to class."

"You still let her go to class?" Adelaydah snapped, glaring at Jason.

"Of course. She is innocent until proven guilty."

Adelaydah snorted, "I don't understand. The victims say they were killed by the vampiress, and she can't remember where she was. How can you think she is innocent?"

"Statements of the dead are not admissible in courts of Eversphere. So I doubt they are admissible in other courts. We need evidence to back up his statement. That is what we are looking for. She is in protective custody right now, as much for her safety as for the safety of others," Mortyiene explained.

"I know where your loyalties lie," Adelaydah snarled at Mortyiene. "I doubt that they are for the health and safety of Sky Village or its inhabitants."

"My loyalties lie with the truth." Mortyiene stiffened her eyes flashing dangerously at Adelaydah.

"Adelaydah, we have not totally ruled out Rhyann as guilty. She is still a person of interest. But we must have proof that she is the one responsible. There is evidence of illusions at work on her."

Adelaydah paused, her mouth opening and closing in fury. "If you will excuse me. Scarlet, I need some air. It is beginning to smell in here. Could you join me?"

"Of course," Scarlet said, glaring at Jason as she rose.

"You know how Adelaydah feels about Rhyann," Boris said,

after the girls had left.

Jason slumped in his seat as the waitress brought his food and drink. "I know. But we cannot arrest her for her war crimes. In fact they cannot enter the picture, save for providing motivation. For some reason, it just does not feel like a vampire attack."

"So what are you going to do?" Boris asked. He used a slice of bread to mop up the remaining mushroom soup at the bottom of his bowl.

"I don't know." Jason took a sip of his soup the creamy texture sliding across his tongue. He took a bite of beef, chewing it slowly.

A scream ripped through the air. Jason and Mortyiene jumped to their feet, and charged out of the tavern with Boris on their heels.

"Mouen oluhjalhau lally." Jason murmured under his breath.

A path of golden light appeared. Jason grabbed Mortyiene's hand, without thinking. He charged through the growing crowd.

He got to the fountain square and saw Rhyann standing over LaFlora. The captain was pressed against Rhyann's body. Rhyann's right arm was wrapped around LaFlora's chest supporting her weight. Her fangs extended deep into the captains neck. Two trails of blood flowed from the puncture wounds. LaFlora weakly struggled. Rhyann's fingers were extended into claws. Her left hand ripped at LaFlora's clothing as blood and tissue ran down her body. A growing crowd of spectators surrounded them.

Rhyann turned two bright orange eyes at Jason. Laughing she slaughtered LaFlora gulping down flesh and blood. LaFlora screamed in agony as limbs were ripped from her body. She then fell mercifully silent.

"Lunlmoun lomll lelolun." Jason summoned forth a glowing ball of minor sunlight. He sent it streaking toward the vampiress.

"Rhyann sopzes," Mortyiene commanded the vampiress. She just laughed at her.

The vampiress hissed as the light streaked for her. She dropped LaFlora's drained body. The sun pursued her into an alley. As

Rhyann fled, she grabbed Adelaydah dragging her deeper into the dark alley out of sight of the villagers.

"Follow me investigator and she dies." The vampiress laughed over the screams of the crowd.

Adelaydah struggled trying to break free. "Help!" Her arms started to bleed from where Rhyann's claws punctured her skin.

"Mistress your magic won't work on me. I have transcended you." Rhyann snarled as Mortyiene tried to command her to release Adelaydah.

Rhyann levitated and flew down the alley.

"Jason," screamed Adelaydah. "Help me!"

As the vampiress escaped down the alley, Jason followed, trying to keep her in sight. He could see an armored Sky Village guard ahead of him.

Behind him, Mortyiene and Scarlet raced to where LaFlora lay.

A bright light washed through the alley-way. Jason threw up his hands to shield his eyes. The flash was accompanied by a crack of thunder. Jason flew backwards. He felt the air rush out of his lungs as he fell onto the hard packed earth.

Down the alley he heard Adelaydah calling to him. Spurred on by her panic, Jason struggled to his feet and ran to her.

He felt for a pulse. It was strong. Adelaydah appeared to be unhurt. Her purple robes darkened from fresh blood that oozed from the wounds on her arms. "Come on. We need to get back to the square," he yelled. "Are you all right?"

Jason and Adelaydah ran back to the square where LaFlora was still barely alive.

"Rhyann, Rhyann," LaFlora said over and over again. "You must... No. Stop, Rhyann....Melegate," she whispered, then stopped breathing, slumping in Scarlet's arms.

Scarlet rose, her red sorcerer's robes darkened from LaFlora's blood. She gently lay LaFlora on the ground and helped Jason gather the limbs that had been torn off.

The caravan guards poured out into the street just as LaFlora died.

"She did it," they yelled. "Why hasn't she been arrested?"

"Mouen lilholn" Jason summoned forth his spectral vision. *"Mouen mouenhau."* He continued, bringing the deep black magic to greater clarity

The area was bathed in deep purple magic along with streaks of grayish red. He whipped out his notebook and jotted down the colors.

"Go and arrest her." A guard ordered.

Jason looked up startled. "I will. She is already in custody as we speak. If she is responsible, she will be punished."

"How could you, Jason?" Adelaydah asked, eyes wide. "You saw her attack. You saw LaFlora's body. You saw her attack me. How can you possibly say she is not the one responsible?"

"Adelaydah..." Jason started to say. "We will follow up...."

Adelaydah cut him off. "You know who did this. You saw. I heard LaFlora say her name. You saw her attack me. You have the evidence, Arrest her now."

The Red Rock Caravan guards grumbled their agreement.

Adelaydah turned toward the gathering mob. "This vampiress killed my village. She killed my people. No mercy. No quarter. Now she is killing people of your village. What do the librarians do? They shelter her. Give her protection."

"We will not protect her if she is guilty." Jason took a deep breath and spoke in an even tone. He was unable to diffuse the situation.   "What's this?" He noticed a strange yellow residue on LaFlora's body. The faint smell of rotting eggs tinged the air. The yellow residue trailed down the alley that the vampire had dragged Adelaydah down. Adelaydah stood on the trail, shouting about arresting Rhyann.

Jason motioned for the peacekeepers to take the body into custody. He pushed his way through the growing mob of citizens, following the trail before it was obliterated.

"If the librarians will not kill her for the murders that happened in their areas, then we should," Adelaydah screamed. Around her the men and women of the guard roared in agreement. Ignoring Jason and Mortyiene, they surged toward The Library. The mob followed the peacekeepers as they took the body to the morgue.

Mortyiene looked after them, startled.

Jason pointed out the trail of yellow leading from an alley. "We must get evidence. We have to do it now. If we wait it will be gone."

Ignoring the stragglers as well as Scarlet and Boris, Jason and Mortyiene entered the alley. They saw a circle drawn in yellow powder. His friends had followed them. Adelaydah had stayed with the mob.

"What is that?" Boris asked, crouching down next to Jason.

"Mortyiene, are there any sulfur springs in the Gloaming close to the school?"

"Sulfur springs?" Mortyiene's asked. She was distracted. "No we have other things to worry about this close to school."

The sound of the mob faded as it drew closer to The Library. He caught her eyes in his and pointed to the yellow residue

"Boris, I have no idea what this is. But it has been present on most of the bodies. The thing did not register vampire to my color sight. It appears that it did not respond to Mortyiene's commands. Though, I was sending a small sun after it at the time, so we are not sure."

"Does that mean Rhyann has other magic at her disposal."

Jason took an evidence bag from his satchel. He could hear the mob at a distance demanding that the librarians bring out Rhyann. Soon the peacekeepers would be there to dispel the mob. He needed to get the evidence safe before that happened.

"I am not sure." He scraped some of the circle into the bag. "But Mortyiene and I need to get back to The Library and soon."

The four of them headed back to The Library. The peacekeeper forces were breaking up the mob. Adelaydah was nowhere in sight when they got to the door.

"I hope she's all right." Scarlet's voice was tinged with worry. She wrung her hands as they wound their way through the press of people.

Jason nodded, also a bit worried that they were not able to find Adelaydah. They pushed their way through the mob to the entrance. Jason and Mortyiene showed their wrist bracelets. The guards saluted his robes and let the four of them in. Jason left Adelaydah's description with instructions she be allowed in the building.

"I need to catalog this evidence. It appears that our evening was cut short."

Boris and Scarlet hugged him. They walked to the lifts that would take them to their rooms.

Mortyiene left for the holding cells to ensure that Rhyann was still there. Jason headed to the LBI processing area. He turned in the sample to be tested by the enchanters and returned to his rooms, exhausted from his "relaxing" evening out.

Chapter 7

When Jason entered his office the next morning, Mortyiene was there at the desk filling out paperwork.

"Was Rhyann in her cell?" Jason asked, taking the cup of coffee that Mortyiene handed him.

Mortyiene smiled. "Yes she was. The guards told me she was there all night and was present during the cell checks."

Jason frowned a moment and then looked at his bookcase. There was a book on the shelves entitled "The Vocabulary of Thaumaturgy." Jason opened it and scanned at the table of contents. "I think The Library is trying to tell me something. What did Librarian Jodian say about Thaumaturgy?"

Mortyiene moved her chair next to his so she could read with him. It book was in a strange language, "Can you read this?" Jason asked.

"Yes this is written in Draconic. This is a teaches people how to summon demons."

Edwardynah leapt into Mortyiene's lap. She sniffed the pages cautiously. "This is a bad book," she intoned, curling up in a ball and submitting herself to Mortyiene's absent-minded caresses.

"This says Gates and Portals." Mortyiene pointed out. Mortyiene brow creased in worry lines.

They turned to the page, "Look," Jason said. "This looks like the same symbols that were in the alley."

"I think we need to go to the thaumaturgy section," she said.

"Why does this book feel weird?" Jason asked absently rubbing his fingers together. "It burns my fingers slightly, like a weak acid."

Mortyiene closed her eyes a moment. "This book was made from a baby's skin. My knowledge of thaumaturgy indicates that the things who create these books use skins and hides of innocents. The magic seeps deep into the skins and draws you in. Every time you touch it, a bit more of your innocence is absorbed by the books."

Jason wrinkled his nose at the thought. "Where do you think we should go in that section? I have a feeling that our bracelets will only be nominally accepted there."

"Jason, let me look at your notes," Mortyiene said. "I want to compare."

Jason took out his notebook and opened to the page where he had sketched the symbols. "Do you see where this symbol differs from those written in the book? That is because this symbol is probably the demon that was summoned."

"So you think," Mortyiene said, "a demon is being summoned and made to look like Rhyann?"

"That is a possibility," Jason said. "Now we have to figure out who is summoning the demon. Which demon is being summoned. And why. That means going to the thaumaturgy section of The Library."

"I know how to get there. It is connected to the necromancy section as one of the draconic based languages. I do know that Rhyann is not the summoner. She is a necromancer, not an illusionist and you said the residual base magic was illusion." Mortyiene looked up from the book. She sketched out the image imprinted on the page.

"Could the demon create illusions." Jason asked. He moved his hands away from the book and fiddled with his pen, flipping it through his fingers.

"I suppose he could, but would not demonic magic look black and red?" Mortyiene frowned and closed the book.

"I don't know much about them." Jason said, putting his notebook away in his brown over-robes. He lifted Edwardynah from Mortyiene's lap and put her in his satchel. Her head peeked out from the brown bag so she could see everything.

Jason got up and headed for the door that lead down to the stacks in the Necromancy section. Mortyiene paused by the main door looking at Jason oddly. "Where are you going?"

"Ah, you haven't seen this door yet," Jason said. He opened the iron-bound door to reveal the stair case. "Come on. This will take us to your section faster."

Mortyiene peered doubtfully at the flight of stairs. "The Necromancy section is down fifty flights. This only goes three."

"This is a librarian's office. Things like space and floors have little meaning here." Jason headed down the stairs making sure his brown robes were in place and his white gold band was showing.

At the bottom of the stairs, Jason opened the door to the strange mirror image study carrel. The layout of the desks and book cases was the same as the main entrance only reversed.

Mortyiene looked out her eyes wide with surprise. "This is so weird, when I started my studies here The Library seemed to draw me to this carrel. But I never saw any door here."

Jason looked around. "It looks like the study carrel where the main door is. I think The Library uses some form of symmetry. Can you see the door now?"

Mortyiene nodded. "It's a little faint, but clear enough now I know what I'm looking for."

"Can you get us to the thaumaturgy section now?"

"Of course," she said. "This way."

Skeletal library cats regarded them as they wound their way through the stacks. Black dusty books on necromancy filled the shelves. Skeletons watched them. The red flame deep in their eyes showed that Bli watched through them.

"Rhyann is a necromancer. The language of necromancy is closely related to Draconic which is the root language for necromancy, sorcery and thaumaturgy," Mortyiene said.

"But I thought that sorcerers were neutral." Jason commented. A library cat hiss at Edwardynah as they walked by it. "At least I am not allergic to skeleton cats." The cat turned and walked down the aisle ignoring Mortyiene and Jason.

"No dander," Edwardynah said, twitching her ears back.

"No dander," Mortyiene said at the same time. "Sorcery is a

neutral language made so by three sorcerers during the wars on Sapphire Islands. They had turned their backs on the dragons and were helping the men and elves," Mortyiene answered.

They wound their way through the extensive stacks. Jason tried not to stare at the books on necromancy. Only some of the titles he could read, Like *"A History of the Great Hauntings in Sapphire islands"* and *"Mathilda the First of the Vampires."*

"I have not studied much on wizardry," Jason said. "It seems like as soon as I got here I was recruited to investigate the murders. I haven't had time to do my own research in the ways of light magic." He paused for a moment to catch his breath. He glanced over some huge mahogany tables covered with stacks of books and scrolls that students bent over, reading and researching. "I suppose once this case is over I might have time for my own research."

Mortyiene laughed as she paused with him. "I have a feeling we are both going to have time to pursue our own independent studies."

"I suppose you are right. You do realize we are now part of the great underpaid civil servants." Jason shoved his hands into the pockets of his over-robes.

"How much are we getting paid?" Mortyiene asked.

"You know, I don't know yet. It never occurred to me to ask when I was getting my bracelet. I suppose we should find out sooner rather than later." He looked down at the satchel and the black and white head of his cat. "Do you know Edwardynah?"

She put her ears back. "Why should I. It has nothing to do with me."

Jason chuckled at her statement. "Edwardynah does not know either."

Mortyiene headed to a stairwell and went down three more floors. The door opened to another section of the necromancy section. Unlike the upper floors this floor was much cleaner. Instead of skeleton warriors there were librarians in black and brown robes. The Library cats were still skeletal in nature, but, unlike the ones in the upper floors, they obviously belonged to or perhaps owned librarians.

"Welcome Librarian," one of the cats said to Jason.

He was startled for a moment. He kept forgetting they were able to talk to him.

"Why don't you have flesh and blood cats?" Jason asked Mortyiene

"We are necromancers. We are more comfortable with the dead than the living," Mortyiene replied.

"I suppose that makes sense in its own odd way." Jason watched the cats stalk through the stacks looking for scroll shrews.

"Ah here we are the door to the Root village administration center. You're right this was faster than using the lifts."

The Root Village administration center was empty, except for a few peacekeepers, the huge doors to Root Village still sealed shut. The peacekeepers lounged about, playing cards. They looked up as Mortyiene and Jason entered, waving to them.

"Do you need an escort Librarian?" Rosliniah asked expectantly. "The men could use a diversion." She said indicating the men sitting at the table. They lounged on their chairs as their swords were hung on the wall behind them. Their boredom obvious.

"I take it, it has been quiet?" Jason asked Rosliniah.

Rosliniah nodded her short cropped dark brown hair bobbing with the nod. "Every since the administration has ordered the doors sealed, the men have been bored."

"We do not need an escort now, but we will probably need one soon," he said, following Mortyiene through another door into the far side of the necromancy section. They threaded their way through the maze of stacks, tables and carrels until they found the door they were looking for.

Heat radiated off the door and Jason felt, more than saw, skeletons following them and standing in silent attention just outside his visual range.

"Bli has sent an army," Mortyiene said, looking down the aisles of bookcases. "They will not follow us into the thaumaturgical stacks but they will remain here."

"Will we need them?" Jason felt his heart leap. He stared down the darkened aisles searching for more skeletons.

"I hope not, but if we do, we will be glad they are here." With a deep breath Mortyiene opened the door and they entered into the first floor of the demonic stacks.

The first thing that hit Jason was the heat. It was like a furnace. It blasted him with the smell of rotten eggs. It was like the heat of the desert all over again. He staggered supporting himself on the door frame that Mortyiene had carefully propped open.

"Why is it so hot in here?" he asked, wishing he had brought water with him.

"I don't know," she replied. "Can you use your sight to find the books that we need?"

Jason shut his eyes and murmured the spell. *"Mouen oluhjalhau lally."*

A bright glowing ball of light jumped from his extended hand and bounced in the air twirling in light blue colors. Jason noticed the books were numbered. However, the titles that he could read were not related to the books closest. Each one was of various size and coloring with no discernible patterns. However, the rows of book cases were clean and shiny. Library cats had glowing red eyes and long fangs descending from their mouths. Their ears were pulled up in sharp points and their scaly tails had snakes heads on them. They hissed in annoyance as Mortyiene and Jason moved deeper into the section.

"Not the most hospitable place." Jason pulled his robes from his chest to create a draft.

"It's so hot here," Mortyiene complained, as they pushed deeper into the books.

The blue ball of light bounced and whirled. It disappeared into the card catalog at the center of the floor. It spun for a moment in front of a drawer and melded into that draw.

"Well I guess we need to use the card catalog. The light will not take us to the book we need. Do you suppose that there is some order here?" Jason asked.

"Only what The Library has established. Even in this section librarians attempt to catalog the books."

"I would not want to be a librarian here. If what I have heard about thaumaturgy is true, then the librarians would not be interested in revealing themselves." He ran his fingers down the front of the card catalog. "Can you find the book we are looking for?"

"The language is draconic so I think I can find it." Mortyiene pulled out the drawer the light had melded into, and flipped through the cards.

"Ah, here we are," she picked up a small piece of scratch paper and noting down the title and the location. "This is a book on the different kinds of demons. It would be nice if The Library just sent you the books that have the information you seek."

"I do not think it works that way," Jason said following her deeper into the stacks.

As they moved down another floor they wove through another labyrinth of books with cats and shadows melding and moving around them. "This is it," Mortyiene said. *"Major Demons of Xalaborn and their Histories."* She picked up the book and handed it to Jason.

Jason's skin crawled as he held the book. It felt like he was holding warm slime. As he slipped it into his satchel a librarian materialized in front of them.

"You cannot take that book out of the section. The cats told me you were checking out a book. It contains some of our deepest secrets in its pages."

"We have no choice we are working on a case." Jason and Mortyiene showed him their bracelets. "We believe that Rhyann is responsible for the attacks. She is engaged in Thaumaturgy and we are looking for the demonic overlord that is responsible." Jason put the flap back over the mouth of his satchel.

Edwardynah's head poked out of the satchel at one end. "This is the investigator you are talking to," she told the librarian.

"Rhyann?" the librarian said, ignoring the cat. "No Rhyann has not been down here to do research."

"Then who has? Surely you must know who the students are that are studying this science." Jason took out his notebook and one of the enchanted pens that never ran out of ink.

The librarian became visibly agitated. He looked around his eyes darting to the deep shadows.

"Who are the current students? It is very important." Jason insisted. He glared at the librarian.

The librarian licked his lips and paused. "Well it is not Rhyann, the only current students are..."

As the librarian reached into his satchel to draw out his list a chant was heard. *"Shax xocxerix axd dessxoyric ixtxudxesixt"*

The librarian screamed. A blazing orange and red gate opened up behind him. A black stork leg appeared followed by the rest of the huge demon. His jet black body the form of a well muscled man and the head was that of a dove. It was covered in gore that dripped on the floor. As it did the stone sizzled and popped. An evil dagger was wielded in one claw-like hand. The evil blade plunged into the librarian's chest. With a mighty wrench, the talons ripped apart the librarian. Blood splattered Jason and Mortyiene as they took flight.

Behind them the cackling laughter of a woman's voice chased them. "Run and hide little librarians I will find you, unless you give up your futile quest to find me."

Jason flung open the door to the stair well. Whispers and hisses filled the air as shadows disengaged themselves from between the books reached for them with unearthly claws. Behind them thundered the huge demonic bird crashing through the stacks, the cries bellowing up through the dark hot air.

Jason felt claws ripping through his robes. Blood poured from his left arm, and his heart pounded in his chest.

Something jumped on his back and cling to it. The claws dug in, gouging his back into deep lacerations. He screamed and slammed himself against a bookcase. The thing attached to his back fell to the floor stunned.

Ahead of them was the entry to the necromancer section. Skeletons, waited, drawn up in a phalanx. Their eyes reflected the unearthly light of Bli watching through them. Jason and Mortyiene charged into the necromancy section slamming shut the door behind them. Skeletons formed up rank and file watching the door carefully in case a demon followed them

Mortyiene and Jason made their way back to his rooms. Even the skeletal library cats of the necromancy section avoided them.

"What is going on?" Jason whispered to Mortyiene. "Why are they avoiding us?"

"They have been ordered to stay away." Mortyiene whispered back. "To not make contact. After the demon returns to its plain of existence the cats will talk with us again."

Once in his office he took out the book and handed it to Mortyiene. "Find something about Shax."

"Shax," she said, tapping her pen against the book.

"Yes I dreamed about him." Jason said, he headed to the bathroom to get first aid supplies. "There was four of them, thaumaturgists, in my dream. The only word I could make out was Shax."

Mortyiene nodded and ran her fingers down the page. "Ah here it is, right here."

Jason shucked off his clothing leaving only his brief's on. He handed Mortyiene the first aid supplies. "Can you work on my back he said."

She divided her attention between his back and the book. "Ah here he is."

Jason hissed in a breath as she dabbed along the deep lacerations. He squirmed under her touch. "Where," he muttered, trying to keep from crying out.

"Here." She pointed to a picture. The same figure that attacked them was drawn in great detail on the page."It says he is a master of deception and medicine..." Mortyiene trailed off.

Jason studied the picture. "It sure looks the same." He took the alcohol and started to dab the injuries on his arms. Mortyiene bandaged his back. Her cool hands felt good on his inflamed back.

"It wants dissected offerings. That would explain what I saw." Jason said, wrapping his arm in gauze.

He studied the scrawling text, trying to make out the words. His eyes rebelled, feeling like hot spikes were pounded in them.

"It sounds to me that an illusionist would be a very tempting target to this demon," Jason said, rubbing his eyes.

"Perhaps," Mortyiene said. "That is one of the most vulnerable disciplines."

"Well, illusionists are mostly human, and humans are notoriously corrupt. I believe illusionists, due to their nature to deceive, are probably easier than most."

A dark red spot fell on the page, and then another. Jason froze and brought his hands to his eyes. He looked at his fingers, now covered with blood, and screamed.

Mortyiene rummaged through the first aid kit. She took out some gauze and padding. She quickly bound up his eyes and led him down to the hospital wing.

"Your eyes are bleeding from the book. It is unable to corrupt you, so it is trying to cripple you," Mortyiene said.

Chapter 8

The emergency room in the hospital wing of The Library was a bustling hive of activity. The riots and the mobs caused several casualties who lay moaning in alcoves. Only librarians, peacekeepers and healers were being allowed out of The Library to retrieve the wounded.

Mortyiene guided Jason into the waiting room. She headed to the clerk's desk. She looked over her shoulder and turned her attention back to the clerk who would check Jason into the hospital

The clerk, the name Nike on her badge, looked up as the black robed necromancer approached, showing the white gold bracelet that announced she was an agent for LBI. She glanced to the waiting area. Her eyes drawn to Jason who was sitting in the there with blood soaked bandages wrapped around his head.

Nike jumped up as she saw the brown robes. She stuck her head through the doors of the emergency department, calling for Penelope. Nike escorted Jason and Mortyiene to a private room. Around them were the moans of the wounded from casualties from sword fights, and magical attacks.

Penelope laid her fingers on his wrist at the pulse point and murmured a spell. *"Namnana Jason'n mumrnmloon, mloommrevvave nennimagfon'nan ann vemneramure ann remormmere."*

The spell spread through his body measuring his pulse rate, respirations and the force in which his blood was pushed through his veins. The bandages were pulled back from his eyes as Penelope looked deep into them. Jason blinked several times at the dim light after the blackness of the bandages. His eyes tried to adjust to the dim interior of the emergency room.

"What were you doing?" Penelope asked, as Mortyiene took a seat in the small cramped room. Penelope was a short plump woman wearing white robes trimmed with blue. A brown apron covered her under robes.

"I am working on the murders that have happened in Sky Village. I was reading a book on thaumaturgy trying to find who was responsible when my eyes started bleeding." Jason's heart pounded in his chest. He felt as if a great weight was pushing down on him. He fought against the urge to rip the bandages from his eyes so that he could see. The moaning, of the other patients, twisted in his gut.

"Did you bring the book with you?" she asked. Her eyes narrowed at his explanation.

Mortyiene fished it out of her bag. "We will need this to finish our research, or, rather, I will. We have to find out what is behind the murders, and why the killer is killing these guards."

"Did you read this book as well, Agent?" the caregiver asked.

"Well yes. But necromancy has the same root base, syntax wise, to thaumaturgy. I was not adversely affected as Jason is."

The caregiver nodded and made another note on her chart. She continued to ask questions for another fifteen minutes. "Diagnostician Lyvinah will be with you shortly. Any allergies, major operations, or illnesses?" she asked, finishing the health history.

"I am allergic to cats. Diagnostician Dunn gave me some lozenges to help with the allergies when I am in my rooms. Other than that nothing." Jason fidgeted with the bandages on his eyes.

"What happened here?" Penelope asked, pulling aside the dressing on his arm and back.

Jason related the story of the attack in the thaumaturgy section. The bandages were pulled back. The deep lacerations flared with a hot searing pain. Blood tricked down his back as the caregiver studied the deep wounds.

"These look infected," Penelope said, her voice tinged with concern. "I will let the Diagnostician know about them as well. Are you feeling any pain or are you cold?"

"No, not really. When you took off the bandages it hurt, but now it is just throbbing. I am a bit cold. May I have another blanket?" he replied.

"I will see about getting you another blanket," she said. *"Wamim Jason'n nlanmet'ym nemormmere nm Jason meln m fenev."* His body warmed as the charm sunk into his chilled flesh. Even with the blanket he still felt cold and was shivering by the time the diagnostician entered the room.

Lyvinah had an easy air about him. His gleaming white robes with red trim, and brown over-robes, designated him as a librarian. His black hair was neatly trimmed. A Van Dyke beard dusted his chin and strong jaw.

"Investigator, I heard your eyes started to bleed after you read a book from the thaumaturgy section of The Library. Penelope also tells me you have some scratches on your arm and back."

Jason nodded, turning his face in the direction of the sound. The diagnostician waved his hand over the enchanted lighting control panel. The light dimmed to a suitable level. "Penelope tells me you have the book. Would you show it to me?"

Mortyiene took it out of her bag and held it up. Lyvinah looked at it and frowned. "Would you open it for me? I dare not touch it. These books are anathema to my school."

Mortyiene opened it. The diagnostician leaned forward peering at the words. He jerked back in his seat. "I can read it, sort of. It makes me want to concentrate on it so I am able to read it more clearly. This is a dangerous book. Please put it away." Mortyiene shoved the book in her bag.

"I am going to take off your bandages so I can see your eyes. I have dimmed the lights to prevent any light damage." The diagnostician gently unwrapped the bandages.

Jason felt something warm and wet slide down his face. He tasted the iron tinged flavor of blood as it trickled into the corner of his mouth.

Lyvinah picked up an enchanted glass that glowed with a soft light. *"Gfnow'lym mu namaghn'ym Jason'm enenovumneen, omn moem Jason'm weegf'lym ne 'amneen mloonme'm,"* he whispered.

Jason felt cool soothing magic at the back of his eyes. The sensation traveled down his tear ducts to the back of his eyes. The nerves tingled as the spell traveled down them to deep in his head.

Lyvinah frowned for a moment, looking through the scope at the damaged eyes. He snapped off the light, and moved over to the treatment cart. The Diagnostician pulled out two eye patches and fresh gauze. He placed them on both eyes and wrapped his head with gauze.

"Well, the good news is that you have no permanent damage. I am going to keep you overnight for some tests and observation. Tomorrow I will send you home unless you take a turn for the worse. The bad news is, you can no longer read that book. During the course of your work you will need to read many tomes like this. We have to come up with a way for you to study them without damaging your eyes."

"What about me?" Mortyiene asked. "Am I able to read the book?"

"You should be ok, in small doses. I have a bigger concern with you though. The bridge between your school and the school of this book." He pointed to her satchel. "Is very small. We have a bigger concern. If you keep it in your possession for too long, you will fall prey to its insidious nature."

Mortyiene took off her satchel and set it to one side. "Believe me, Diagnostician, I have no intention of looking at this book for one second longer than I must."

As Lyvinah left the room, he said. "I will send a caregiver in to get you transferred to a room in the hospital. I think you have some more paperwork as well before then."

Two signatures and a few questions later Jason was resting quietly in his room. He was prepped by Penelope for a series of diagnostic teasts. A tubal scope, created by medical enchanters helped the diagnostician see inside Jason's head. This would give a detailed picture of what was going on inside of his head. Lyvinah would be able to see if there was any permanent damage. Jason was grateful Mortyiene stayed with him. Her presence calming him until she was chased out of the tubal scope room when Lyvinah was ready to run the tests.

* * *

Mortyiene stood in the observation room while Jason was in the tubal scope. Her fingernails made half moon indentations in her palms. She was sweating despite the coolness of the room.

Lyvinah had been with Jason while he was in the tubal scope. He had ordered Mortyiene to stay in an observation room. He put his hands on the tube that Jason was in. The machine hummed and whirred. A light flashed in the view port. The diagnostician peered through the view screen. He made notes on Jason's chart from time to time.

After twenty minutes, Lyvinah entered the observation room.

"No permanent damage," he told her. "The bleeding has all but stopped. I want to keep him overnight for observation."

Mortyiene nodded. Penelope pushed Jason's wheel chair back to his room. She helped Jason into bed and read two scrolls, one promoted healing his eyes, the other to help him sleep.

Mortyiene sat with him until he drifted off holding his hand. When she heard his soft snore she bent over and gently kissed him on his forehead.

"I do not know what I would do without you," She whispered, and left his room.

She caught up with Penelope at the caregiver station. "He is asleep. I need to report this to Laurel. If he awakens tell him I will be back tomorrow."

Penelope acknowledged her, and Mortyiene walked out of the hospital.

Mortyiene mused a bit on her way to LBI headquarters. Who was behind the attacks? Why were they targeting Jason? Would he be able to see clearly or had the book done some permanent damage to his eyes? The necromancer wound her way through the desks to Laurel's office. She knocked on the door and waited to hear the come in.

Laurel stood up when Mortyiene entered. She motioned for Mortyiene to sit. The Director started to prepare tea in a small self heating enchanted pot. Mortyiene thanked her and sat in the chair.

"Would you like some tea, Agent?" she asked, taking out two cups.

Mortyiene nodded and sank deeper into her chair.

"How do you take your tea?" Laurel asked, scooping three spoonfuls of tea into the pot.

"Two sugars," Mortyiene said, gripping the chair arms.

Laurel finished the tea and handed Mortyiene the cup. Mortyiene's hand shook as she stirred the brew.

"Jason is in the hospital. We think we have figured out who or what is killing the villagers."

"Oh really." Laurel looked up from her cup of tea.

Mortyiene related their trials of the evening. "We need to retrieve the body of the librarian that was killed by that creature."

"I will send two peacekeepers. What are you going to do now, Agent?" Laurel said, scribbling notes on her pad.

"I thought I would take my friend Lucero with me to Root Village. See if I can find a lead as to who the thaumaturgists are."

Laurel said, "we have an uneasy truce is happening between The Library and Root and Sky Village over this damn vampire. Why did she have to come on my watch?"

Mortyiene laughed. "Rhyann had reached the end of her syntax capabilities. The channels needed to open for the next round of vocabulary and concepts."

"I know why," Laurel muttered. "It is just that she is over five hundred years old. Now she is involved with the war. Her powers are waxing. Why now? Why not in thirty years? I would be dead and gone and the next administrator would be dealing with her."

Mortyiene regarded her boss coldly. "She is a hero in our

country. She destroyed an enemy town with no cost to our own soldiers. Secured our outpost. What is one people's villain is another's hero."

Laurel jumped at Mortyiene's words. "I am not used to hearing your side of things. Perhaps Bli is right. We have become too hidebound in our way of thinking. We have forgotten that your side of the war has its own people and hero's, just like the River's Alliance. My apologies Mortyiene, I was unkind." She looked down and stirred her tea.

"Does this mean I can stay?" Mortyiene leaned forward in her chair, her tea cup forgotten in her hand.

"I am not sure, but you do bring interesting insights. Go on. Get your friend and learn if there are any thaumaturgists in Root Village. I look forward to hearing your report."

Mortyiene rose and set her tea cup on Laurel's desk, leaving the office. The lift carried her down to the cells and apartments of the students from the Draconic Alliance.

Lucero was in his room studying an enchanting text when she knocked. "Want to go out for a night on the town?" she asked, leaning against the door frame.

"Sounds like a plan." He closed his book and headed for the wardrobe, his deep brown eyes sparkling.

"Meet me at the entrance to Root Village in forty five minutes. I need to clean up a bit." Mortyiene said, watching Lucero opened the wardrobe door and study the various gray robes that hung there.

Mortyiene closed the door. She went to her own apartments two floors down and took off her working robes, setting them in the laundry hamper for Bina, her maid, to clean. Bina, a pretty slave girl on loan from Root village, hovered over her.

"A bath first," Mortyiene said, but do not wash my hair. I will wear the sequined robes, and I want my hair braided."

Bina took out the elaborate robes, brushing off a small piece of lint. She gently bathed Mortyiene, keeping her hair above the water. She toweled down her mistresses gleaming white body, and draped the skin hugging robes.

Mortyiene loved how they draped from mid thigh to the floor. A small string of sequins swayed along the tightly strapped bodice. She sat while the maid braided her hair in a complex crown and weave. Mortyiene stood looking at herself in the full mirror.

"Well done girl." She watched the slave girl bob her head up and down happily. "While I am gone clean my other robes. Then have your dinner. Stay in the apartments in case I need you again. When I return I will need my hair unbraided."

She twisted her body to look at her back, as Bina held up a small mirror. Mortyiene checked the back of her head and approved of the style Bina had created.

Mortyiene headed down to the entry to Root Village where Lucero was already awaiting her arrival.

Lucero stood at the door the door to Root Village. His well built body was enhanced by gray robes that accentuated his broad shoulder and narrow waist. The guards and Lucero let out a collective breath at her entrance. She shimmered in the light, reflecting her own dark presence. Lucero bowed over her hand, his lips briefly touching her gloved fingers.

"My lady," he whispered. "You look stunning."

She gave a throaty laugh. "Considering that I will be asking questions I thought it would be better if I put on the trappings of my rank."

Desiderio, the barkeep, scurried from his place behind the bar the moment Mortyiene and Lucero entered the room. He materialized from behind the counter to personally seat them in a cozy corner near the fire place. He shooed the previous inhabitants and deftly cleaned off the table and chairs. Mortyiene glided into the seat with her back to the corner. This left Lucero in the more vulnerable position.

Much like Sky Village Inn had Gloaming food, The Root Cellar had Rivers food, including baked trout with sweet grasses and mushrooms, the non Gloaming variety. Mortyiene loved fish. She seldom had it while traveling under on the great underground continent. The few fish that were present, in the depths of the earth, were generally poisonous or foul tasting. She had not had fish since she left Eversphere.

Lucero, equally thrilled to have Sky Food, ordered a thick beef stew.

As Desiderio hurried off to get their orders, Mortyiene told Lucero about what happened. "We need to find out who the thaumaturgists are," she said, sipping the delicate chilled white wine she had ordered with the fish.

"You think it is someone from The Draconic Alliance?" He took a swig of his deep nut brown ale.

"It is most likely. After all, it was Pegasus Cove soldiers who were attacked. But something is odd." She paused a moment. "It seems to be attached to what happened in Melagate. Which is why so many people seem sure it was Rhyann. These were soldiers from the River's alliance that responded to the attacks on Melagate."

"We are a poor choice for demons to corrupt," Lucero added. "If the legends are true our souls do not offer much sustenance, but our kind can read those books easily enough."

"This demon is very powerful. I saw him coming from a gate. A lord of this caliber simply would not respond to a call from someone already in the black arts. We just do not have the soul energy that would slake his appetite"

Lucero nodded and took another sip of ale. "What if it was someone from River's Alliance? That would be a tasty bit of soul meat for the demon."

"That is what I think. I still want to follow up with the tavern keeper to find out if he has heard if any thaumaturgists are in The Library right now." She paused and glared at the table next to her. She watched the eavesdropping patrons return to their conversation.

The owner personally brought their food, leaving Mortyiene

and Lucero to enjoy their meals. They thanked him and enjoyed the well prepared food from The River's region.

A harpist took the stage and played songs of love and honor--of blue skies and green grasses. Tones were hushed throughout the pub as men and women ate and listened to the talented harper. A peasant couple, that farmed the mushroom fields outside Root Village, got up and danced when the tunes turned lighter. Mortyiene found herself smiling and tapping her foot to the music.

The tavern keeper returned to the table and Mortyiene leaned toward him. "I need to ask you some questions," she said, showing her bracelet to the Desiderio.

He motioned for them to follow him to his office.

"Do you know of any thaumaturgists in The Library or from the Draconic Alliance?" she asked, skipping right to the heart of the questioning.

The tavern keeper closed the door on the revelers and turned back to her. "Aside from those chosen by The Library to work that section, there are four thaumaturgists here right now." He leaned closer to Mortyiene. "And one of them is from The Rivers region. I saw the four of them here together and overheard them speaking about their project."

"Do you know who they are?" Mortyiene asked.

"The three from the Draconic Alliance are Kriston, Hok and Tyree. I do not know who the other one is. Kriston will be leaving tomorrow to return to his home and Tyree arrived the other day. Hok showed up two days ago, right before the attack on Sky Village."

"We need to speak to Kriston tonight. Maybe he knows the name of the thaumaturgist from The Rivers."

"Perhaps. When I saw the four of them together they didn't use names. I think those that make deals with the underworld are not inclined to share their upper world identities with each other. I just know she was wearing purple robes."

"She. Are you saying she was a woman?"

"Yes, and she appeared to be the leader. My guess would be the demon she signed a contract with is quite a bit more powerful than the ones the others made deals with."

Mortyiene noted the names of three men the tavern keeper recognized and looked at Lucero. "We need to speak with them tonight if able. I do not want to wait until Jason is out of the hospital. Those that dabble in thaumaturgy are seldom long for this world."

Lucero waited while Mortyiene paid for their dinner. Desiderio protested, stating it was an honor to serve the LBI, but Mortyiene insisted. "The doors to The Library are closed. This has caused decrease in patronage from the students. You need the money." She pressed an Eversphere silver coin into his hand and left the cheery tavern with Lucero.

As they passed a darkened alley, of which there were many in Root Village, a shrouded figure in black hailed them. "The price has been paid. There will be no more killings unless you continue to push," said a deep masculine voice.

"Who are you? Why have you done this?" Mortyiene turned toward the voice. Next to her Lucero knelt down on the cobblestones drawing a circle with a bit of chalk.

"Do not test me necromancer. The price has been paid. Already more deaths than needed have resulted from your meddling." The voice echoed from the shadows.

"Are you one of the four thaumaturgists Desidero was telling us about?" Mortyiene took out her notebook.

"Desidero talks to. much. Leave off your investigation and no one else dies." The shadow rolled on itself, separating from the wall.

Lucero started whispering the strange liquid language that sounded, to her ears, the same as Jason. She knew he could not respond as quickly. The diagram in the dirt flared up and a glowing ball of deep blue light started bouncing toward the voice in the alley.

"Xoxxosxia of poxshax dexxsoyrix" A deep black pentagram radiated heat and darkness that repelled the light globe that Lucero had summoned. Shadows molded into the forms of imps and detached themselves from the wall. With an abyssal cry they streamed from the alley toward Mortyiene and Lucero.

Mortyiene barked out a spell. *"szaiszes sifeshaz."* Her sickly green ray glanced harmlessly off the detached shadow. Before their eyes the shadows melded and formed into a large demon. As the imps molded and joined in osmotic fashion, the form grew larger. Eyes sprouted over the deformed body. Six arms and four legs erupted from a membranous sack spewing green ichor over the alley. Mortyiene pushed Lucero away from the beast.

With a careless swipe it batted Lucero's light ball back at them, and oozed down the alley way. The smell of rotting eggs choked Mortyiene. She struggled to breathe.

With chaotic laughter, it took another swipe. Hot and cold burned them simultaneously as the appendages found their targets. Lucero howled in pain and the glowing ball dissipated.

Blood dripped from the claw marks, as Mortyiene grabbed Lucero's hand. "Run." She pulled him after her. They ran as fast as her tight robes would allow. Her heart pounding in her chest from fear.

Behind them the thing gave chase as Mortyiene and Lucero sprinted for the door to the library. A couple of Gloaming Caravan guards moved to intercept the thing chasing them. The Library door loomed ahead of them.

Mortyiene felt the thing almost upon her. Her robes hindered her. The side seams on her robes stretched and split apart as she ran. With her legs freed, she sprinted the final distance to The Library door.

Lucero was breathing hard and blood streamed freely from the claw marks. Already black lines radiated from the lacerations.

Crap, she thought as she charged through the door to The Library.

Peacekeepers poured out of The Library. The thing was upon

them. The superior weapons sliced through its amorphic flesh, while superior armor protected them from the viscous claws. With a puff of smoke, that smelled of rotting eggs, it was banished back to the underworld where it had come from.

Lucero collapsed on the floor near Mortyiene, having a hard time breathing. She whipped off his belt and tightened it around his thigh to prevent the poison from reaching his heart.

"Take him to the hospital," she ordered, flashing her white gold bracelet.

Two of the peacekeepers saluted and brought out a stretcher. They lifted Lucero onto the stretcher and headed to the lifts that would take them to the hospital wing.

Mortyiene patted Lucero's hand. "They will take good care of you. I need to change and hopefully mend these robes. I need to talk to the people that Desidero said were thaumaturgists."

Lucero held her hand briefly. Then he slipped into unconsciousness. The lift arrived and two peacekeepers carried him into the lift which rose silently to the hospital wing.

"Well that settles it," Mortyiene said to the duty sergeant. "I need an escort. I must question a couple of suspects. They are both in The Library. I would appreciate someone to stand guard with me."

The desk sergeant made a note on his clipboard. He motioned to Chesmue who was standing close by. "Accompany the agent back to her rooms and then go with her as she conducts her interviews."

Chesmue arose and gave Mortyiene a rakish green. He was a Blaschkar, a tiny man not much taller than her mid thigh. His black and bronze striped body blended in easily with shadows cast by flickering flames. Two small swords were strapped to his waist.

Mortyiene sighed surveying his tiny frame. I wonder if Jason would get a more imposing guard, she thought as she waited for the lift. The lift rose smoothly to her floor and she entered into her apartment. "Wait here."

She called for Bina. "I need my other work robes, the ones that are clean. I need my hair replaited. When you are done repair these robes for me as well."

Bina's deft fingers followed her mistress's command. Mortyiene found her polite and capable. She would have to purchase her from her owner after this case if she stayed in The Library.

Her hair was rebraided into a high tight bun that she preferred when working. It stayed out of the way, while still being protected. She sometimes grumbled that she was the hardest working lady of quality in Eversphere. Most of the girls of her caste and age lounged around and gossiped. However, since she developed the syntax for necromancy, she had to work. That meant extra steps to protect her hair.

She desperately wanted to stay at The Library. If she returned to Eversphere her father would, sooner or later, make her companion. Her friends back in Eversphere chatted about their upcoming companioning ceremonies. They looked forward to the food and festivities and wondered what kind of men their father's would choose for them. Mortyiene wanted nothing to do with that. She was happy single. If her family made her take a companion it would mean children, and that would mean her athletic form would become soft and pasty like her mothers. It was her goal to prove it was good for the bureau to keep her on as an agent.

She left her rooms, and motioned for Chesmue to come with her. They headed to Tyrée's room in the student cells. She knocked on his door and waited for an answer. She heard crashing and felt the peacekeeper loosen his sword.

"Who is it?" A call came from the other side of the door.

"LBI, We have some questions to ask you," She replied, holding her white gold bracelet to the peep hold.

The door unlocked. Tyrée looked out at Mortyiene. "How can I help you, Agent?"

"Desidero identified you as a thaumaturgist. I need to ask you a couple of questions," she replied.

"I am not one. He is mistaken." Tyrée's knuckles grew white as he clutched the doorframe.

"Listen, three guards and a librarian are dead because of thaumaturgy. If you choose not to answer these questions I will assume you are guilty and arrest you right now. The way Sky Village is acting I doubt they will much care if you are the one responsible or not."

He opened the door wider allowing Mortyiene and Chesmue entrance. Chesmue's slipped through the door. His brown and black striped body blended with the lanterns light.

She looked around the small cold bare room. This was the standard dorm rooms for Draconic Alliance students. Mortyiene wondered if those of the River's Alliance had better quality rooms.

Her eyes trailed over the tomes in his bookcase including three on demonology. She pointed to his shelf. "If you are not a thaumaturgist, why have you checked out these books?"

"It is not illegal anywhere to study thaumaturgy." Tyrée shuffled from one foot to the other.

She leaned forward, bringing her internal authority to bear. He recognized her caste as one of the highest in Eversphere. It was his home as well. "No it is not. It is illegal to kill someone here or at home."

"I have not killed anyone. It is her. She killed them," Tyrée blurted out.

"Who is she?" Mortyiene leaned forward. She pressed her body up against his. She trailed one gloved finger down his cheek.

"I do not know. She always goes veiled. She has not revealed to us her name. She is strong and powerful. Much stronger than she should be for The Library." Tyrée jerked his face back from Mortyiene's touch.

"What do you mean?" Mortyiene's face hovered over his. Her breath ruffled his hair. She forced him to meet her gaze.

"I mean, I think she already went through the chamber and opened up the next level of syntax. Working with her is heady, and such a powerful demon answers her calls." He took a step back and stumbled on a lip of stone. He fell back against the wall.

"Do you know the name of this demon?" Mortyiene pressed her advantage. Her left hand flat against the stone wall. Her right hand continued to trace his cheek bone.

Tyrée shook his head. "No I don't. She made spells to prevent me from revealing its name. She makes offerings of autopsies. It revels in deception. I think she is an illusionist because one time I saw her in purple robes. This was at the beginning, when I first got here. Since then she has worn black robes. Of course if she is an illusionist, it would not be hard to make her purple robes black. Would it?"

Mortyiene shrugged. "So you have no idea who she is?"

"Only that she is from The River's Alliance. I think she started this study for revenge or retribution. She seems to think she can stop at anytime." He shook his head.

"Why are you shaking your head?" Mortyiene's finger closed around his mandible. She forced him to meet her eyes.

"Well the problem with this school is that you cannot stop. Your patron will not allow you to stop. I made a choice. Our armies are not squeamish about using demons. In order for my family to be safe, and to get a promotion in caste, I purposely chose this life. She, I think, was tricked."

"Tricked how?" Mortyiene brought her face closer. She breathed on him, her breath cool. She could feel her black energy pour through him.

"Well, she seems to think she is in control. Though she must know that selling her soul to summon it for revenge has a cost. It seems like some of the areas of thaumaturgy she is just innocent about." He pressed against the wall, trying to get away from her.

Mortyiene released him. She took out her notebook and made a note. "Thank you Tyrée. You have been very helpful."

She left the room and stood out in the hallway a moment reviewing her notes. "Come on two more witness to speak to. It is time to speak to Kriston."

Chesmue nodded and followed Mortyiene. He struggled to keep up with her, so she slowed her steps a bit, allowing him to catch up.

Kriston was the son of the nobility caste, even higher than Mortyiene. She found his rooms on the apartment floor. His apartment was similar in design to hers. He answered the door fairly readily.

"Desiderio, at Root Cellar, told me you were studying thaumaturgy. We are wondering if you know the name of the fourth thaumaturgist." Mortyiene dove in. It was best to be blunt with the nobility.

Kriston closely inspected her bracelet and studied her hair. "Military or nobility?" he asked in return. His dark brown eyes met her black ones.

"Agent as far as you are concerned," she replied. "I ask the questions."

"My father will hear of this when I return to Eversphere."

"Do you understand what using Thaumaturgy is? What the costs are? I can see why Tyrée uses it. He is trapped in a lower caste and only wants to move up. But you are of the nobility. What motivation could you have to make deals with the underworld." She took out her notebook.

"That is none of your business. As for the fourth one, I do not know her name. I do know she is an illusionist. One time, when we were casting a spell, I heard her use Illusionist syntax. I know--because, I am an illusionist." Kriston leaned against the doorframe.

"So you know for certain she is an illusionist, and female." Mortyiene looked up from her notebook.

"Without a doubt. She tries to conceal her robe colors from me. But she does not know that I am one as well. Illusions often are clear to other illusionists. She is powerful. Soon she will be able to summon illusions that can kill on their own without the need for demonic intervention. I believe the lord she works for allowed her that little self-deception. Now he has piggy-backed into her magic. He puts his own touches on her illusions. So when she thinks she is done he will be firmly entrenched in her work."

"Thank you, Your Eminence. I appreciate your feedback," Mortyiene said, closing her notebook.

Hok's room was silent. He was located down near the tharlion pens. The great lizards stirred in their pens. They averaged six feet tall and walked on their hind legs. Their front legs were stunted and useless. The rank piles of tharlion manure and moldy straw made Mortyiene's nose wrinkle. The peasants that worked the mushroom fields gathered the manure and tilled it into the dry rocky soil.

Unlike the students in The Library proper, the natural science students lived outside the walls of The Library. They had a private entrance into the courtyard. This offered them rooms with windows that could open. They were however even more sparse than the cells the lower caste students used in The Library proper.

Mortyiene knocked on the door. A single candle gleamed through the window. "LBI, Hok open up," she shouted, holding up her bracelet.

The room was silent. The candle flame flickered. "We know you are in there. Open up," Mortyiene commanded.

Still no answer. She stepped back and motioned Chesmue to open the lock. The blaschkar took out a packet of tools and deftly opened the lock the door slid open.

Hok stood at the back of the room, eyes wide and wild. "I did not do anything," he cried, shrinking back from Mortyiene and Chesmue.

She stalked toward him floating like a shadow. "I know who you are." She trailed one gloved hand down his cheek. "You were in jail in Eversphere. Fraud, I do believe." Her fingers stroked his cheek.

He turned his head away from her. Chesmue slithered close to her, drawing a sword, ready to jump in if she needed it.

"Is this how you survived. You made a deal and now you are a slave?" Mortyiene whispered.

"Please Mistress, it will do worse than kill me if I tell you anything." Hok shuddered, pulling back from her touch.

She encircled his throat with her hand. *"Zanshirshaz Zissyas,"* she whispered. She threw her head back, feeling warmth and energy drain from him flowing into her.

Her pale skin flushed as she drew her attention back to the man who trembled under her touch. "One more time of this and it will kill you," she murmured. "Tell me. Who is the fourth thaumaturgist."

"I don't know her name," he whimpered. "Only that she is from Pegasus Cove. That is all I know. She has kept her identity covered. But I saw her once in the entry hall."

"Would you recognize her if you saw her again?" Mortyiene cooed, reveling in the terror and despair that flowed off the man in her power.

He nodded, pale. "Y...yes Mistress," he whispered.

Mortyiene stepped back and let him go. "Thank you. I will need to speak to you later to identify her. If you see her around I expect you to come to me right away."

She swept from the room, Chesmue right behind her.

"You don't mess around do you Agent?" He grinned, playing with his dagger. They headed back to the main building of The Library, dodging puddles and piles of manure.

"Sometimes being direct has its advantages. I wish I could convince Jason of this."

"Normally agents and investigators do not resort to torture. They find it unreliable."

"As do I. The promise of torture is usually enough, and he was much more cooperative after I reminded him who I was.

She shut her notebook and made her way back to the hall. "I am done for the night. I have the information I need. I will return to my quarters and write up my report for the evening."

She turned on heel and headed back to her rooms, taking the stairs the two flights up to where people of her caste were housed. Once there she sat down and started her report on what she found and information she had.

* * *

Jason lay in the still dark of the hospital room. The door to his room was open. He heard Penelope at her station. Every so often she came in and asked how he felt. She gave him a capsule with some water to swallow it and murmur. *"Jason malgiream yumle 'ym meoulream nerJason n'eneovum"*

She put her fingers lightly on his eye bandages.He felt a warm presence in his eyes relieving his light pain. She patted his hand. "Try to get some sleep," she murmured and left the room closing the door behind her.

Jason dozed fitfully when he felt another presence, cool as the morning mist.

The figure stood over Jason for a couple of minutes. The sound of a dagger being drawn was very clear to his sensitive ears. Jason felt for the chord, that rang a small bell at the caregiver's station alerting her that a patient needed her. He felt rather than saw or heard the dagger plunging toward his heart. He rolled off the bed. The blade plunged into the mattress where he had lain just a heartbeat before.

A feminine voice cast a spell. *"Thloothth oth thaphothshgh dexxsox wixx xonxxt xnixfe 'x."*

The sound of Penelope running to his room reached his ears.

Jason listened, trying to get a name from the phrase, but no names were used. The smell of rotting eggs filled the air as a gate formed on the other side of the bed. Penelope burst in just as a figure jumped through the gate. With a thunderclap it closed. Jason felt the top of the bed and touched the hilt. It burned his skin. He wanted to rip off his bandages and look at it. He leveraged himself up and swayed.

"Get this to the LBI offices. Let their enchanters study it. Find me another room. This room is now a crime scene."

Penelope nodded. She took his arm leading him to another prepared room. Two peacekeepers stayed behind to guard the area that Jason had inhabited just a few heart beats earlier. The black dagger radiated black and red light that pulsed with each heartbeat of the two guards standing watch.

Chapter 9

The following morning Lyvinah examined Jason's eyes and back, and declared he was cleared to leave.

Jason blinked as he got used to the light again. While he dressed Mortyiene told him about the night's activities.

"We need to question the witnesses to the attacks yesterday. The ones that saw what happened before we arrived." Jason winced as the soft material of his blue robes rubbed against his still fresh lacerations.

"We should get some peacekeepers to help us. I am not sure I want to go outside The Library without them." Mortyiene turned her back to Jason as he dressed behind a screen.

"I don't want more than a couple of peacekeepers," Jason replied. "The people of Sky Village do not need to be scared or threatened anymore than they already are. Enough of them have been killed in the last few days, including a decorated veteran of the Rivers-draconic war. It is time they think we trust them at least as much as we trust Root Village."

Jason and Mortyiene left The Library, Chesmue and Elifelet in tow. Jason flipped open his notebook, and consulted his notes. "Jardon saw the attack. He witnessed it. Let us find him first."

Mortyiene fixed her veil in place when they left The Library. Her eyes shone like bright black portals above her black veil. "He was the general store owner, wasn't he?"

Jason, Mortyiene and the two peacekeepers threaded their way through the hustle and bustle of the early morning traffic in Sky Village. Several citizens had camping gear hoisted on their backs, while they awaited permission to leave in the caravan. Citizens were trying to escape Sky Village.

The shop was full of people attempting to buy supplies. Jason noticed a broken window was boarded up. He waved over a stout man with a jovial smile on his face. With a nod to the lady of the establishment, Jason showed his white gold bracelet to Jardon, the shop owner. "We need to ask you a couple of questions." Jason followed the man to his office located off the main floor."What happened to your window?" Jason asked, making a note in his book.

"It happened during the riot. Is the vampiress going to jail?" Jardon's face was red. His eyes sparkled and gleamed.

"Not sure. We are still trying to get statements about what happened and gather more evidence." The two investigators sank into the seats offered to them.

"Well, I was walking home when I heard something in the fountain. From the alley, the vampire flew into the square and tackled the woman. It was awful. Blood was everywhere, and all LaFlora could do was scream." Jardon reached behind him and brought out his jacket. "I saved this for you. The blood spattered onto my clothing as well."

Jason put Jardon's jacket into the evidence bag. "When the vampire attacked LaFlora, how did she do it?"

"Well, that's the odd thing." The man started pacing around his tiny office. "I mean, I don't know much about vampires. But I did not think a vampire attack would be so violent. It must use up more energy to kill your prey in that fashion than you could ingest. Everything I read about them said vampires are gentle killers. But I have seen pictures of Rhyann, and it was her. I'm sure of it."

Jason made a notation in his book. "So let me get this straight," he summarized the shopkeeper's statement. "This vampire attacked like a violent predator, not what you imagine a vampire attack to be like?"

The shopkeeper nodded. "But it was Rhyann, I am sure of it." He leaned forward. "I got a glimpse of her when she checked into the school a few days back. I wanted to see the Butcher of Melegate. It was her all right. I'd stake my reputation on it."

Jason frowned a moment and made a note in his book. "Who pointed her out to you in the lobby?"

"Oh, one of the students from Pegasus Cove. She wore purple

robes. Adelaydah I think she was called. Talk to her, she knows what Rhyann looks like."

"Thank you for your time." Jason closed his notebook and rose. The two investigators left the general store. Jason stopped for a moment and looked at his partner. "Did that seem a bit odd to you?"

Mortyiene stopped in the street. "What he described was not a vampire attack. Yet he is quite sure that Rhyann is responsible. I am not buying it. Rhyann is over five centuries old. I have heard of younger vampires losing control. However, those attacks are never on just one person. When a vampire loses control, they tear through many people until their thirst is slaked. It is like she wanted to be identified. Plus we know she did not leave the detention area. We have guards that provide an alibi that she was in her cell all night."

"Could she have not mesmerized the guards?" Jason asked, studying his partner carefully.

Mortyiene shrugged. "I suppose she could have but why would she make such a spectacle of the attack. Why would she attack a student in front of so many witnesses. Rhyann is not that stupid."

Jason paused, looking down at his notebook. "Shae is next on our list." He turned to Chesmue and Elifelet. "Do you know him? Apparently he is a retired peacekeeper."

Chesmue and Elifelet looked at each other. "Yes, we know him. He is old but still sharp," Elifelet replied. "He sees everything in the village. We know where he lives."

Shae was an elderly man who lived in an apartment above the street. He was not able to move as quickly as he used to. He had put in over thirty years as a peacekeeper for The Library and the librarians. The peacekeepers frequently used him to supply information and witness accounts. Chesmue led the group to Shae's rooms overlooking the alley where the attack took place.

"Saw the attack I did," the old man said. "I know my daughter has declared that I'm losing my mind, but I tell you I saw what I saw." Shae wheezed and took a deep breath from a mask that he held over his nose and mouth. It was attached by a long tube to an enchanted box. Vapor swirled from the mask when Shae took it from his face.

"What did you see?" Jason flipped open his notebook.

"A flash of black and red light. The light lit up the alley clear as day. I saw the vampire step out of the portal."

"Are you telling me that the vampire used a portal? Had you seen one like it before?" Jason wrote down what the man said.

"Can't say as I have. However, there are only so many ways the Draconic alliance can enter Sky Village. One is through The Library, one is from the desert, and the last is through some kind of portal or teleportation of some fashion."

"Was there anything else that was odd about this vampire?" Jason fixed the old man with a steady stare, his pen held over his notebook in anticipation.

"Listen young'un, I was a peacekeeper for over thirty years. Ain't nothin' natural about that vampire attack. Twenty-five years ago a rogue vampire took to the streets of Root Village and started a killing spree. Before the peacekeepers and the guards of Root village stopped him he killed over twenty people. But none of the crime scenes were as violent as what I saw the other night. Vampires lull their prey into a sense of security, then they die. They are simply not that violent, even when they are rogue and driven mad from hunger."

"Yet," he continued. "I saw Rhyann step out of that portal, or should I say she charged out of that portal. It was her. I have seen her in The Library doing research and I saw her check in. It is just odd. The use of the portal. The violence of the attack. The smell-- like rotten eggs. Vampires typically don't smell. If they did, their prey would be scared off."

Jason thanked the man and closed his notebook, tucking it away in one of the pockets of his robes. He got up to leave and Mortyiene followed him.

"He's right you know," Mortyiene said. "Vampires don't smell. You and I smelled the rotten egg smell in the alley. Also, Rhyann is a necromancer. She does not have the power of teleportation or gating. That is a limited specialty unique to enchanters and thaumaturgists."

"Do you think Bli could have created the gate?" Jason asked. "The guards told you Rhyann had not left her cell all evening."

"I doubt it. He is a necromancer as well, though I am fairly sure with his thousands of years of life he might have learned the basics of other schools. I doubt he has developed enough in the language syntax to create something as complex as a gate. Enchanter gates are permanent. They require both the end point and the starting point to be inscribed and spelled."

"We are back to thaumaturgy." Jason rubbed the space between his eyebrows and chewed on his lower lip. "But who is responsible? What is behind these attacks? Is Rhyann being coerced or forced to do these attacks against her will?"

Mortyiene regarded Jason evenly. "When we find out the answers to those questions I think we will find our killer. If Rhyann is indeed being forced to do these kills by, say a demon, does that mean she is going to be held accountable for them?"

"I am not sure. We will have to ask Laurel about that. But let us talk to the third witness to find out what she saw."

Yanaba was a guard for Red Rock Caravan service. She witnessed the attacks, and chased Rhyann down the alley when she fled, holding Adelaydah as hostage. Her dark-brown hair tumbled over her deeply tanned skin. She had a bow strung over her back and held a clip-board checking off cargo to be loaded onto the camels. The caravan would leave in the evening, and the camels would be loaded closer to departure time.

"When the vampire ran," she said, "I was close. I drew my sword and was ready to attack her."

"Where did she go?" Jason made a note in his book. "I know the peacekeepers tried to follow her, but she had disappeared."

"That's the odd thing." Yanaba looked up from her clip-board and motioned the next traveler to come forward with their luggage. "I saw a dark-cloaked figure and heard chanting. I had never heard that language. It had a lot of hard sounding x's like 'axe.' When she was done chanting, a great burst of black and red light filled the alley and the vampire charged right into it. Did not slow down. The gate closed just as a yellow ball of light as bright as the sun streaked into the alley. The figure I saw chanting the words vanished as well. All that was left was the illusionist that the vampire had held hostage."

"So someone else was in the alley? Did you see who it was?" Mortyiene asked.

Yanaba shook her head. "No. By the time my eyes cleared and I could see in the alley she was gone. But I know it was a woman. The voice sounded female."

"Could this woman be working with Rhyann?" Jason looked up from his book so he could see the guards reaction.

"I'm not sure. I do know whoever is behind this attack has an accomplice." Yanaba motioned for the next passenger to come forward.

"If I were to get someone who could speak the language you heard, would you be able to identify it again?" Jason moved out of the way, as a family of four approached the table and laid their bags on it.

"I'll never forget it. It made my skin crawl. I never want to hear it again. Most of the languages I have heard in and around The Library, even the languages of necromancers, do not affect me that way. It was truly horrifying. If words have the power to horrify you."

Jason nodded and thanked the woman. He and Mortyiene left the Red Rock Caravan office and headed back to The Library. Their two peacekeeper guards looked relieved at the uneventful investigation in the village.

* * *

"We need to talk to Adelaydah," Jason said, after bidding farewell to Chesmue and Elifelet. "Perhaps she can tell us if it was Rhyann or something else. After all, it did take her prisoner."

Jason glanced about the hospital wing as they entered it. Penelope was still at her desk, having gotten some sleep in the early hours of the morning when everything was quiet.

"We need to see Adelaydah," Jason said. "Is she up for visitors?"

"Of course Investigator. I just changed her dressings. She should be released tomorrow." Penelope guided them to Adelaydah's room. "How are you feeling?"

Jason flexed his arm and shoulder feeling the slight pull from the recently healed scratches. "A bit stiff, but on the mend."

Adelaydah was sitting up in bed with a bulky dressing around her neck and shoulders. "Did you arrest Rhyann yet?" she demanded as they entered the room.

"That is what we wanted to ask you. Are you sure it was Rhyann?" Jason asked, his pen poised over his notebook.

Adelaydah looked up, her eyes flashing in anger. "Of course I am sure. I would never forget that face. I will always remember it. It killed my parents, my brothers and sisters. How could you think I would not recognize it?"

"Tell me exactly what happened," Jason said, sitting on a chair next to her bed.

"You were there, you saw it. After she finished with LaFlora, she grabbed me and was going to kill me. If you and the others had not chased her down the alley, she would have killed me too."

"Why did she not kill you?" Mortyiene glided into the room and stood next to Jason. Her black eyes fixed on Adelaydah's face.

Adelaydah ripped off the dressing and Jason could see the wound in her neck and shoulder held together by tiny stitches. "She tried. She would have succeeded if Jason had not been there.

I want to press charges. I want her to pay for the death of LaFlora and the assault on me. It is my right, as long as I am a student here in The Library, to press charges."

Jason stood up snapping his notebook closed. "We are gathering evidence against her as we speak. This case is not that easy, but, Adelaydah, I promise we will bring whoever is responsible for this attack to justice."

"I told you who was responsible. Now leave me. I am tired and I need some sleep." Adelaydah turned to look out the window her back to them.

Jason and Mortyiene returned to the caregivers station. "How bad were her wounds?" he asked Penelope, who was busy charting.

Penelope looked up and down the hall. "You know I cannot say, Investigator. The patient has a right to confidentiality."

"A creature's life is at stake. If we are going to find justice for those that died I need to know how serious Adelaydah's wounds were," Jason demanded. "Perhaps a warrant from the magistrate will smooth things out."

Penelope looked at the two of them, and their white gold bracelets. "Her wounds were not that deep. Mostly superficial. It was more bloody than fatal. If the fangs had bitten her just a quarter inch closer they would have severed her carotid artery. As it stands it was just messy. She responded well to treatment and antibiotics."

"Did she smell like anything?" Jason asked, jotting down what Penelope said.

"Now that you mention it, she smelled like rotten eggs. I thought that she was poisoned by a toxin. But, her blood tests came back clean for sulfur poisoning." Penelope flipped through her chart.

"Sulfur poisoning? Is that common?" Jason asked.

"Not very. But we do get it from time to time. Mostly from people that get lost in the desert. They are driven mad from thirst and drink from a sulfurous pond. Generally though, people stick to the caravan routes and travel with the caravans." Penelope looked up from the chart laying open on her desk.

Jason thanked Penelope. He and Mortyiene left the hospital wing. "Interesting. Another one says that the vampire smelled like sulfur. I think Adelaydah was mistaken."

Mortyiene agreed. "Perhaps the enchanters have identified the smell. It will be interesting to see what has caused it."

The lift rose smoothly to the enchanters floor. As it pulled to a halt, the door slid open. They came face to face with an irritated Edwardynah.

"You wind up in the hospital from reading a book-- You get attacked in the middle of the night-- You don't bother to tell me about it." She demanded. Her tail twitched back and forth.

"Sorry Edwardynah. My eyes started bleeding and Mortyiene took me to the hospital. I was attacked there last night. I just got released this morning and I was out interviewing witnesses from LaFlora's and Adelaydah's attacks. Now I am on my way to the enchanters lab."

"Which is why I am here. A messenger came by and wanted me to tell you that the Enchanters had some results. I knew you would be heading up here next. I'm coming with you." She turned and headed down main hall way to the laboratory. Her tail held erect.

Mortyiene chuckled and followed with a sheepish Jason in tow.

Professor Malor, the head of the enchanter's lab, was a great rotund man. He had sparkling green eyes that twinkled from under a mop of curly brown hair and a bright red face. "Investigator, it is good to meet you. I have the results from the tests you asked me to run."

Jason shook the man's hand. "Nice to meet you as well. So tell me what have you learned."

"The easiest thing to test was the yellow residue. It has similar properties to sulfur, but it is not sulfur."

"What do you mean?" Jason asked, taking out his notebook and poising his pen above it.

"It is brimstone. It is not naturally occurring. It does not exist on this plain of existence." Professor Malor gestured expansively. He looked like a magician revealing the final component of an illusion.

"If the victims were killed by thaumaturgy, would it leave that residue?" Jason asked. His heart leapt in his chest.

"I believe so. Keikanne told me that the scorpions that attacked you in the desert were mutated and also covered with the yellow residue. Whatever is hunting you is not of this plain, and is certainly not a vampire."

"And the blood?" Mortyiene looked at him questioningly. "Does the blood have the anacolang enzyme?"

Professor Malor's face broke out in a wide grin. "We were lucky with that raid. Several raiders were killed by the vampire. Those that were killed in the village were killed by something that looked like Rhyann. The ones we know for certain that Rhyann killed did have the anacolang enzyme. Where as those that were killed in the village did not. Furthermore, those in the village, killed by whatever was out there, had the brimstone residue on them. "

"That means..." Jason started.

"... that something is disguising itself to look like Rhyann and pretending to be her, but is not of this world." Mortyiene smiled. Her body slumped in relief over the news.

* * *

"Come here," Jason said as they left the lab. He directed them to a table along one of the side aisles. He took out his notebook and began thumbing through the pages."Look here, you said that whoever the fourth thaumaturgist is was wearing purple."

Mortyiene nodded. "That is what Kriston said when I

interviewed him."

"Illusionists wear purple. Furthermore, a powerful enough illusionist should be able to disguise his or her voice and that of any demons that were summoned." Jason pinched the bridge of his nose. His skin flush from excitement as he voiced his thoughts.

"But Jason," Edwardynah interrupted. "That is graduation powerful magic. Unless the illusionist was a librarian, they would have returned to their home cities."

"Not necessarily," Jason continued. "What if he or she snuck into the Mana Chamber before their classes. The early opening of their channels, combined with the demonic influence, allowed the illusionist to cast more powerful spells than normal. This could mean that the illusionist is a student here... right now."

"We need to speak to Marge," Edwardynah said.

Mortyiene looked puzzled, following half the conversation. Jason translated, "Edwardynah is telling me that the level of illusion was so powerful that they would no longer be a student here."

"I agree with that, Jason," Mortyiene said. "We need to find out who the students are, and soon. These murders are recent."

"Then let's get a list from Marge. Edwardynah told me she is the one to speak to."

They took the lifts back down to the main entry hall. "There she is." Edwardynah twitched her tail, pointing toward a huge woman with bleached blonde hair piled high. Her flabby jowls and chins jiggled as she talked, and the three of them headed for her station.

"Jason Litweiler, LBI," Jason said, showing Marge his white gold bracelet. "This is my partner, Agent Mortyiene Bakon. We need some information."

Edwardynah leapt lightly to the counter. She sat primly covering her feet with her tail.

"I need the current list of illusionist students," Jason leaned against the counter.

"Of course Investigator." She hauled out a huge tome and quickly wrote down several names. "These are the current illusionist students and librarians in The Library at this time."

Jason thanked her and headed to one of the tables and sat down. Twelve names were on the list. Next to the librarians was a checkmark.

"I think we can rule out librarians for the moment. Look, here is Kriston. You told me he was a thaumaturgist, but he said he was not the leader. So let's keep him as a person of interest. Adelaydah is on the list. I think we can rule her out since she is from Pegasus Cove. That leaves Hadwin and Xacob."

"Hadwin is the second administrator of Eversphere." Mortyiene peered at the list. "Questioning him will be difficult. I do not know who Xacob is." Mortyiene drew the list to her. "Not many illusionist students in The Library right now. Do you think one of them is the fourth thaumaturgist?"

"No time like the present to find out." As Jason stood to go and find the students, a librarian trotted up.

"Investigator. It was hard to find you. Laurel requests that you meet her in her office, right now."

Jason looked at Mortyiene and Edwardynah. "We were on our way to question some people. Can this wait?"

"No sir. She insisted right now."

Jason put his notebook back in his robes along with the list of illusionists. The three of them headed for the stairs to the LBI floor.

Jason knocked on Laurels door and entered when he heard the invitation to come in. Three nomads were in the office with Laurel. Sarad, the leader, sat in one of the blue upholstered chairs, his back very straight. The other two stood by the door their arms crossed. Laurel sat at her oak desk her spectacles perched on the top of her head. Her brow furrowed in concentration.

"Jason." Laurel looked up as the three entered the room. "Mortyiene, Edwardynah, I am glad you could make it. You remember Sarad."

"Of course." Jason bowed over clasped hands. "How can I help you? We have a lead we were about to follow up on."

"Sarad was telling me how impressed he was with you when you visited his camp. You recognized their traditions and investigated the bodies without dishonoring them. He has called a temporary truce to the hostilities. It could be made permanent if you can find out what is preying on his people."

"We don't want to be at war with The Library. You are the first whose come to our camps to see for yourself. It's seldom that the librarians travel beyond the walls of your building. To take the time and see the damage whatever plagues both our homes brings us hope for a better future." Sarad stood and returned the bow over clasped hands.

"Of course Sarad. I believe what attacked you is tied up in what is wrecking havoc the desert. We have evidence that great magic is at work. I will let you know who or what is responsible, when we have concluded our investigations."

"That is all we ask of you Investigator. Now if you will excuse us we need to return to our camp. This building presses down upon us like a weight. We need to see the sun and the sky to be at home." Sarad said, a smile playing upon his dark features.

With that, he bowed low, once again, to Jason and Laurel. He swept out of the room his clansmen in tow.

"What have you learned?" Laurel asked.

"At the enchanter's lab, we discovered that the yellow residue was not sulfur, but brimstone. It has been present on a number of dead bodies and was on the scorpions. We believe that a demon is acting like Rhyann. It disguises itself through illusions to appear like the vampire, and kills people by biting their necks. This means illusionists. We were about to question the illusionist students, when you called me into your office."

"And you believe this demon is also responsible for the troubles in the desert?" Laurel put her spectacles back on, knocking one of the pens out of her bun and onto the floor.

"It may very well be that those that think they are controlling it are unaware that it is corrupting the desert. The demon is just using them for his own purposes."

Laurel looked at the list of students and Librarians. "I know most of these librarians. I do not believe they are part of this. Start with the students, then let me know what you have found."

Jason nodded. The three of them filed out of Laurels office.

Chapter 10

Jason paused outside Laurel's office. "I think we should question Hadwin first. He might have the biggest grudge against Pegasus Cove."

"Hadwin! You want to interview Hadwin?" Mortyiene's shocked voice startled Jason.

"Sure. He is an illusionist from Eversphere. He seems a likely choice." Jason eyed her, wondering why she was so resistant.

"Well, it should be interesting. I will let you take point on this one." Mortyiene glanced about the room, not able to meet Jason's gaze.

"Why?" He lifted an eyebrow, trying to catch her eyes.

"He sat on the Uver's high council for over fifty years. Hadwin is one of the most powerful men in Eversphere. I, personally, would rather not insult him. But I will make the introductions, of course. Let us hope he is in a good mood today." Mortyiene hauled out her own notebook. She flipped through the pages still not looking at Jason.

Jason shrugged, and wondered why Mortyiene was so elusive. "Well, if you know the way, lead on. The registry roles says he is in the Uver's suite. Do you know where that is?"

Mortyiene marched to the lifts that would take them deeper into The Library. A short while later, a mere single floor above Root Village, they stood in front of a door with two Eversphere guards.

"We are here to see Hadwin." Jason held up his bracelet that identified him as an investigator.

Mortyiene showed her bracelet as well. She remained very still as the guard inspected it.

Satisfied, the guard commented, "we'll see if he's receiving visitors. He's not well, of course."

Jason whispered to Mortyiene. "Are those official Eversphere military?"

"Yes, he is entitled to full military escort," she whispered back, her body tense and straight.

The guard returned from his inquiry. "You may enter."

The palatial rooms stole Jason's breath away. There was even a window overlooking the vast mushroom fields surrounding Root Village. Crystals sparkled in the rock of the huge cavern, like a field of stars.

Hadwin stood to greet them. "Librarian. Mortyiene. Do come in. Would you like some coffee?"

Mortyiene glided forward and knelt on one knee, and pressed the ring on the old man's right hand to her forehead. "The eye sees everything."

"The eye protects us from all who would destroy us," the old man responded.

He motioned for Jason and Mortyiene to sit on the plush couches. Edwardynah leapt onto Jason's lap.

"So what brings you to an old man on this chilly day?" He motioned for his servant to bring in the coffee.

Jason sat on the couch as a slave brought in a steaming pot. "We are questioning all illusionists. We believe an illusionist is responsible for the deaths of three Pegasus Cove guards, several villagers and a Librarian."

"And you think I am behind it?" The old man gave a wheezing laugh. "You are right, young fellow. I am an illusionist, but I am not responsible. On the day LaFlora was killed I was here, in my suite, hosting a dinner party for eighty guests."

"Well, could you not have summoned an illusion to fool the guests?" Jason took a cup of coffee made richer with real cream and sipped it. The hot liquid warmed his limbs, and he felt it all the way down to his toes.

"Look at the Mana Chamber records. You will see that it was just today that the next layer of syntax was opened for me. I am still suffering from the effects, so I could not even summon a likeness of myself right now. I am an old man who is just now studying the

154

magic." The old man took a cup of coffee from the servant. "The spell that you describe would have to be from someone who has opened the second level of syntax. The grammatical concepts of the spell would be too complex for anyone with just a Mountain syntactical awareness."

Anger washed over Jason. Why were people resisting his investigation? If they had nothing to hide, why wouldn't they just tell him what they knew. "Perhaps, but I know that you have seen many battles. Maybe you wanted LaFlora and her team dead from a loss you suffered. A son or daughter perhaps." Jason sipped his coffee.

He spoke in the calm measured manner of someone who spent a life-time in politics."Yes, I must admit that the thought of killing Pegasus Cove soldiers would be of great interest to me. My son was killed in the Battle of Char's Neck, so the thought of killing those soldiers would bring me some peace. But at what cost? The neutrality of the schools is of paramount importance to me. Already Pegasus Cove uses them too much for their own political purposes. The chambers would be destroyed if Eversphere were to move directly against them. No, son, it does not benefit Eversphere to kill those soldiers. We have too much to lose. Already the librarians and Sky Village are demanding the closure of Root Village-- and want to deny Eversphere students entry to The Library. The peace is tenuous at best. I would not kill a soldier of Pegasus Cove in any of the schools. You must find the one who benefits most from the destruction of Pegasus Cove soldiers." Hadwin leaned back in his chair.

"And the time that Yule was killed? Surely sir, you cannot expect me to believe you were hosting yet another banquet?" Jason asked, frustrated. The old man was wily and evaded his questions. It was difficult to remain polite.

The old man chuckled. "I find it amusing, Librarian, that you would believe an old man, such as I, could be spry enough to be appear to be in a different location from my body and create an illusion, and that I am energetic enough to summon both the illusion and a demon. The night that Yule was killed I was in the hospital wing. I will give permission to the caregivers to release the information about my stay. The road to The Library was arduous. I did not handle the travel well. I do not look forward to my return trip. The dry air here suits me, and I shall stay until my strength returns. I have a personal Diagnostician and Caregiver. They accompany me everywhere. I fear, however, that old age has no cure." He steepled his fingers. His cloudy blue eyes fixed on Jason and Mortyiene.

Jason noted the man's whereabouts and thanked him for his time. He and Mortyiene left. "You were awfully quiet during the interview."

"I found it safer for my family to let you do the talking. He is not a man that suffers invasions of his privacy lightly. He is still one of the closest advisors to the Uver." Mortyiene glanced over her shoulder at the two guards standing outside Hadwin's door.

"What was it about the eye?" Jason flipped through his notebook, finding the greeting that Mortyiene and Hadwin had exchanged.

Mortyiene looked at him silently for a moment and then said simply, "it has to do with our banner, that is all. Who is next on the list?"

"Xacob Edinborough." Jason read from the list Marge had given him. "Let us hope he is more cooperative."

"Never heard of him, are you sure he is from the Draconic Alliance?" Mortyiene peered over Jason's shoulder at the list.

"His room number indicates so. He is in your student dorms. It just means he is not part of the River's Alliance." Jason handed the list to Mortyiene so she could read the room number.

Mortyiene nodded, "Aye. We, like you, open our dorms to those that do not fit into our sphere of influence."

Xacob was in his room studying when they knocked on the door. He wore red pants and a yellow tunic, the colors of Good

Fellow island. A tall man, an eye patch covered the twisted scar of the left eye he lost in battle.

"I am not really part of the Draconic Alliance, but the people of Pegasus Cove do not approve of the pirates of Good Fellow Island. So, when I am in school, I stay with the Draconic students." He crossed his arms and glared at Jason with one angry brown eye.

Jason nodded, making a note of this in his notebook. "So where were you two nights ago?" He met Xacob's gaze steadily as anger welled up in him again. Maybe I will be taken more seriously when I am older, he thought.

Xacob thought for a moment. "I was in the Root Cellar entertaining the crowd. I needed money for my stay here. Sometimes I perform illusions for entertainment." He continued glaring at Jason with his one good eye.

"And two nights before that? Where were you?" Jason could not keep the anger from his voice. Another dead end he thought.

"Ah, that one is easy. I was in the damn desert making the final trip to The Library. We did not get here until after the soldier had been killed. Though I was here for the raid," Xacob replied.

"Have you used the Chamber yet?" Jason watched Xacob, his pen poised above his notebook.

Xacob shook his head. "Not yet. I am due to use it in three days. I am still taking classes on what to expect with the more advanced syntax. Then I will return to Good Fellow Island"

"Is there anyone that can vouch for you two days ago?" Jason scribbled down what Xacob had told him.

"Aye. The tavern keeper at the Root Cellar. He hired me to perform for his patrons." Xacob stroked his chin for a moment. "Desdario was his name."

"Have you ever studied Thaumaturgy? I am sure a demon would be of great assistance to a pirate." Jason looked up from his notebook, studying the big pirate.

"Thaumaturgy? No, I have not. Dodgy things those demons, and we sailors are already too vulnerable to the whims of the seas.

We are not inclined to make deals with things that are notoriously fickle and are happy to do us in for their own amusement." He paused for a moment. "No benefit for us to make deals with demons. We steer away from them."

Jason looked at the slip of paper from Marge. It verified that Xacob was not in the school on the day that Yule was killed. This also meant that he could not have disturbed the scorpions, since he had indeed arrived the morning before the raid. Jason thanked Xacob and left the room with Mortyiene.

"Do you think that we are on the wrong track? That possibly the killer is not an illusionist?" Jason asked.

"I think that you need to accept the fact that we need to look at Adelaydah. She has motive and opportunity." Mortyiene stopped outside of Xacob's door.

"What is her motive for killing Pegasus Cove soldiers? Especially those that came to her village's aid after the attack by Rhyann." Jason glared at Mortyiene. Adelaydah could not have done this, he thought. She lives in Pegasus cove.

"Hopefully, the military records will be here soon. That might shed some light on why." Mortyiene made a note in her own book. "The other illusionists have been ruled out. We must consider her a person of interest."

Jason chewed his lip thoughtfully, a habit he had picked up from Mortyiene. Adelaydah, he had known her since The Mountain. She was always cheerful and helpful. He was so wrapped up in his own thoughts he did not notice a shadow detach itself from the wall and follow them back to his rooms.

Chapter 11

The next day dawned in the cool confines of The Library. Jason stretched his limbs, enjoying the feel of clean sheets and the warmth of a fire in his bed chamber. He sneezed, a sign that Edwardynah had, once again, disobeyed orders to stay off his bed. He peered down to the foot of his bed, frowning at the library cat who was working very hard at ignoring him while she was taking a nap. He moved his feet under her, trying to shove her off his bed, without much success.

"Stop that," said a miffed feline voice. "You're disturbing my rest."

Jason got up, pulled on clean robes and the supple brown leather over-robes, belted everything, and slung his satchel over his shoulder as he headed down to the cafeteria.

Scarlet was in line already. Boris and Adelaydah were not in evidence. He grabbed a plate of eggs and bacon and filled his mug with deep, rich coffee. Even if he got nothing else from working for The Library, the coffee was worth it. They had it at Pegasus Cove, but it was expensive. Here it was more common but still a treat.

Scarlet sat at their usual table and started on her breakfast. "So how goes the investigation?" she asked, delicately nibbling on a slice of melon.

"Ok, I guess." Jason twirled his fork around in the fried potatoes.

"What is going on?" Scarlet asked. Of everyone here, she had known him the longest. They were babies together. Her family and his family had history as far back as he could remember.

"Something is bothering me. I am hoping you can help me out." Jason stuffed potatoes and egg into his mouth, unable to meet Scarlet's gaze.

"Spit it out Jason." Scarlet set down her fork and studied him.

"It is about Adelaydah. Has she ever, you know, disappeared

without telling anyone?" Jason swallowed took a drink of coffee to wash it down.

Scarlet burst out laughing. "Adelaydah, Adelaydah.... You are not serious?"

Jason stopped and looked at his childhood friend. "Scarlet, I have to be. We know the one responsible is also an illusionist. There are only four illusionists in the whole school right now, and the other three have been discounted. That leaves Adelaydah. Has she ever taken off or left your house with no good explanation?"

Scarlet paused, frowning a bit at the question. "Well, she does go to the orphanage to help the kids that wound up there from the attack. Other than that, she has not left."

"What do you know about the attack on her village?" Jason lifted another bite of breakfast to his mouth. The yellow yolk of the eggs mixed with the crispy fried potatoes.

"It came on quite suddenly at night. Rhyann and her minions had made their way through ten houses before any alarm was raised. Adelaydah managed to conceal herself and ten kids in the temple to Ishkatar. By the time the vampiress was forced to flee there was only Adelaydah, the kids and a wounded woman."

"When did Pegasus Cove soldiers get there?" Jason wiped his fingers on a napkin. He pulled out his notebook and wrote down what Scarlet said.

Scarlet frowned. "By the time the soldiers arrived and started to fight Rhyann, almost everyone was dead. You know Adelaydah never speaks much about the attack, or the soldiers that came to their aid. I have often wondered what happened. Why it bothers her so much."

Jason finished his breakfast when a very cheerful Adelaydah joined them. He glanced at her. "I thought your syntactical synapses had been opened yesterday. Why are you so cheerful?"

"I must be lucky," Adelaydah said. "Not even a twinge of a headache. Unlike how I felt after the Mana Chamber in The Mountain."

"Well, I need to report there for my own appointment. Take care you two." Jason put his tray in the scullery room and trotted off.

* * *

Travian, the librarian responsible for the Mana Chamber, was an enchanter. His gray robes showed up neatly under his brown librarian over-robes. Penelope was also present to give aid. Occasionally, during the course of having new grammatical pathways open, a blood vessel would burst. As a result a caregiver was required to be on duty anytime a student went in.

The door to the room was never locked as Root Village sent its own representatives to help their citizens through the arduous process.

Jason was asked to remove his librarian over-robes and leave the satchel in the waiting area, before going into the Mana Chamber. The natural cave formation, located a few floors beneath the surface, was filled with pink and green crystals that formed spider web patterns throughout the walls.

"Close your eyes," the librarian advised him. "It will be easier."

Jason sat on the comfortable chair and propped his feet up. The door to the cave slid shut. The room started to hum. Though his eyes were closed, the flashes of light still hurt. In his mind he could hear complex wizardry sentences. His limited vocabulary opened. He saw and heard the words strung together, forming more detailed incantations. New spells flooded his mind. He clenched the arms of the chair as conjunctions, definite articles, indefinite articles, prepositions, adjectives and adverbs flooded his mind. Vocabulary he did not understand sprawled before him in a multicolor palate of light.

As he lay fighting the pain that pounded in his head. Something slithered into his thoughts. A black shadow pulsed in synchronization with the flashes. He screamed in agony, clawing at his temples, trying to call his magic. But it would not come. He slid from his chair, his ears bleeding as pain wracked his body.

Suddenly, the Mana Chamber dimmed and the lights in the crystals faded, and the room darkened once again. The shadowy presence retreated, leaving him bleeding on the floor. He opened his eyes, seeing two doors open.

Penelope sprinted to Jason's side, fumbling with her bags. She took out a set of orders, and placed her cool hand on Jason's temple. *"Me nh'lym nhe namaghn'mo mloom'lym ne mnegfllym."*

Warmth spread from his temples through his head. The pain lessened. He sat up, wiping the blood that flowed from his ears and nose. "What happened?" he whispered.

"Take it easy, Investigator," Travian said. "Something followed you into the chamber. It attacked you during the opening of your new channels."

Jason blinked and the two Traivan's melded together. Penelope sat back on her heels, watching him carefully. Blood hammered in his temples, and he winced at each heart beat.

"Follow this," she said, holding up a finger.

Jason tracked, it blinking several times. She peered deep into his eyes, flashing a light to test his reflexes.

"You gave us quite a scare. I want you to check into the hospital if you have any complaints of pain." Penelope put the scrolls and the magical light into her brown leather caregiver's bag.

Jason agreed and took a couple of tablets she provided to help with the pain. He belted on his over-robe and headed to the lift that would take him back to his suite in the wizardry section.

* * *

Mortyiene's day started like most. She arose. Bina helped her dress. But today Mortyiene knew that Jason was going to the Mana Chamber. He had studied vocabulary deep into the night. She decided that it was time for a trip to The Root Cellar.

With the nomads declaring a truce, and Rhyann locked in protective custody, the door to Root Village was open once again. She sniffed the cool, dark air with faint undertones of Tharlion, mushrooms, and grave dirt.

She headed down the main street. The stores were open, selling their wares. Several students were shopping, including some she recognized from the Rivers Alliance.

She sat in a darkened corner in The Root Cellar, her text books out in front of her, learning more vocabulary for school. She saw Kriston enter and take a table not far from her. He wore black robes with red runic trim. His hood was pulled up, but she could still identify him from his walk. Desiderio caught her eye and jerked his head in Kriston's direction.

Kriston ordered some food and glanced in her direction, his eyes passing over Mortyiene like she was not there. He finished, paid his tab, and skulked out of the building.

Mortyiene shoved her books in her bag and followed him out the door. He paused for a moment, looked up and down the streets, and headed for The Library.

Mortyiene continued to follow him. He darted down a lesser used street and broke into a run. She turned the corner and saw him sprinting toward an intersection. She ran after him, her boots heels clicking on the cobbled street.

She rounded another corner and ran straight into a grotesque caricature of a locust. It was as big as a warhorse with a twisted humanoid face and a barbed stinger on its tail. Three of them lay in wait for her. She saw Kriston continuing to sprint down the street. She turned, fleeing from the demons.

One of them leapt from their pack and landed in front of her, swiping at her with a hooked claw. She screamed and ducked, darting down a side street, fear speeding her on.

Chittering in excitement, they followed her in great leaps. Their huge bodies thudded on the street. She felt the lane vibrate each time a locust demon landed. She screamed again as she reached the main thoroughfare.

Around her men and women shrieked. The Root Village Militia responded to the noise. They streamed from their posts, drawing themselves up in a line of steel. Dim elf rangers shot arrows at the things. Mortyiene scrabbled down the main street running for The Library.

Behind her she could hear the slaughter. Men and women screamed as the numbers of the mutant locusts swelled. She looked over her shoulder. What had started out as three demons had swelled to at least fifteen. She sprinted toward The Library, calling for the peacekeepers. They streamed out and rushed down the street to join the battle.

When the peacekeepers formed up their own line and advanced on the warhorse-sized mutant locusts, she stopped and turned to the advancing insects.

"Si'shijj shinvias seszrayas," she yelled.

A black wind, blacker than the perpetual night of The Gloaming, burst from her hands. It whirled in a malevolent maelstrom. She willed it over the peacekeepers that had formed a wall of steel and advanced on the demonic locusts.

The creatures ceased their slaughter, trying to grasp onto the smooth stones of the street. With a howl, the violent wind yanked them up and flung them into the black tornado. Men and women fled from the raging necromantic wind. With an ear-splitting thunder clap, the mutated locusts were destroyed.

With a thud, their bodies slammed back onto the street. Black blood pooled under their broken bodies. Mortyiene put her hand against a wall to steady herself. She could barely stand. The world whirled about her as she bent over and vomited.

"Agent, are you all right?" Rosliniah put a rock-hard arm about Mortyiene's waist.

Mortyiene looked up and wiped her mouth. "Yes. I am sorry I caused you concern. That is the first time I used that spell."

"Do you need to go to the hospital?" Rosliniah pulled her

closer, and Mortyiene leaned on her strong frame.

"I will be all right. I just need to rest. Go and see if the people need medical attention."

As peacekeepers went to assist the wounded, a voice hissed through the air of Root Village. "I speak now to Mortyiene. I warned you to leave me in peace. Yet you follow my minions and hound me at every step. Cease your investigation and no one will be injured. Already, Jason lies bleeding in the Mana Chamber. It will only get worse if you do not leave me in peace."

Mortyiene stood and shouted into the air. "You must be held accountable for the deaths and injuries you have visited upon the people of the villages and The Library. Jason and I cannot allow you to continue. You must pay for your actions."

Around her people glared at her. Men, women and children lay wounded in the streets. "It's not my fault," she yelled. "Leave me alone." She fled back to The Library, her boot heels echoing through the hostile blackness of Root Village.

* * *

Mortyiene waited for Jason in his office with a folder in her hands. "We got the military records this morning. Laurel just sent them up."

Jason blinked, trying to see her clearly. "You better read it, I am not able to focus."

Mortyiene's face twisted in sympathy. "Oh... You were in the Mana Chamber this morning. I will be going this evening with the Draconic Alliance. I am not looking forward to it."

She opened the folder and read along. "Ah, this is interesting." She held up a sheet that had most of the lines blacked out due to security concerns. "It appears that both Yule and Shang were going to be court-martialed shortly after Melegate. Instead, the military let them resign without honor. Let us find out what happened."

"This is terrible," Mortyiene continued. "They were to be

court-martialed for looting and raping. There were several of Rhyann's minions still in the village when the Pegasus Cove soldiers arrived. In the aftermath of the battle they found a woman and raped her to death. The soldiers all claimed she was one of the invaders. It turned out she was a surviving villager." She paused a moment, frowning. "The victim was raped in front of the screen that Adelaydah put up to hide herself and the children. LaFlora was their captain, and tried to cover it up. However, Adelaydah brought charges and demanded punishment." She pursed her lips a moment before continuing. "A healer that specializes in counseling told the military that Adelaydah's state of mind was traumatized, so she exaggerated what had happened. It would be better to discharge them without honor. LaFlora, because she covered for her soldiers, was also forced into a discharge without honor."

Jason leaned back and whistled. "I guess we have motive. Adelaydah must have witnessed the looting and raping. What does the rest of the record show?"

Mortyiene lay the pages she had read on the desk. "Apparently Shang and Yule were not the most exemplary of soldiers. LaFlora was. She served with distinction in several battles. She won the Pegasus Cove Star of Valor for her action in the Battle of Char's Neck, where she singlehandedly held off a durrock advance. She sacrificed her pension and her career to keep those two out of jail."

Jason steepled his fingers thinking about LaFlora. "She was captain of the guards on our caravan." He leaned forward and picked up one of the sheets of paper that Mortyiene had placed on the desk. "This would explain why she was fighting with Shang and Yule when she finally arrived. Was anyone else involved in this gang rape and looting?"

Mortyiene looked at the report. "Apparently there were five more. They died under mysterious circumstances in Pegasus Cove. Three from disease, Bayou Malaria to be precise. The healers were not able to treat it." She paused, looking up at Jason.

"Bayou Malaria? That is from the Black Bayou. I did not know it was common that far south."

"It is not." Jason held a paper at arm's length, trying to focus on the words.

"Well, it says they were part of an expeditionary force into The Black Bayou. The healers had inoculated them. What does that mean?" Mortyiene looked up from the paperwork.

"Healers in Pegasus Cove have a way of healing before someone gets sick. The treatment mimics the disease, but in a milder form so the body recovers easily, then is immune." Jason gave up on trying to read the papers. Instead, he stroked Edwardynah as she lay on his desk taking a morning nap.

"Oh." She paused a moment. "This is interesting. Apparently the inoculations didn't work. The other two were killed by alleged vampire attacks, also while still in Pegasus Cove. Shang, Yule and LaFlora had, by that time, joined the Red Rock Caravan company and were gone."

Mortyiene continued to scan the report. "Hey. You were the lead detective on the last vampire kill."

"Tell me the dates of the deaths." Jason wiped a trickle of blood that ran from his nose. "I am not sure, but I think those are the dates Scarlet said Adelaydah was away from the house." He rubbed his temple, fighting the headache from the Mana Chamber. "I have to ask Scarlet again to be sure. But it appears that all of these deaths correspond with the days that Adelaydah was visiting the orphans."

"We need to detain Adelaydah and not allow her to leave The Library." Mortyiene grabbed a warrant request from a drawer. She looked at Jason, raised her hand as if to pat his arm, and then let it drop into her lap. "I am sorry, Jason. I know she was your friend."

He was emotionally drained. He slumped at his desk. Tears, unbidden, came to his eyes. "Adelaydah," he sighed. Adelaydah had been his friend for nearly ten years. He remembered when she came to Pegasus Cove to live with Scarlet's family. She had always been so nice, a wonderful companion, willing to help. Yet all along she had been behind the deaths of these soldiers.

"I guess when she saw Rhyann here she decided to pin the murders on her. I wonder how long she has been studying thaumaturgy?" Jason wiped his eyes with his handkerchief and sneezed. "Damn cat," he said.

Mortyiene leaned back in her chair. "I would guess since shortly after the raid. She was still in Melegate at The Mountain. It was her illusions that kept the kids alive." Mortyiene shook her head. "To have witnessed the guards of Pegasus Cove killing a villager. It must have given her abyssal lord the opening he needed to send her over the edge."

Jason rubbed his temples again, then stuffed his handkerchief back in his pocket. He reached for the arrest warrant. In a clear, neat, deliberate, hand he wrote out the name Adelaydah Clayton,. He affixed his seal, stood, and walked to the door, with Mortyiene close behind.

"I am going with you," Edwardynah said. She trotted after the pair as they left the office.

Chapter 12

"We will need back up," Jason said, as they left his office. "Let us see if Rosliniah is available. I am not sure how dangerous Adelaydah is.

Rosliniah was in the peacekeepers' barracks and agreed to come. "Give me a few moments to assemble a team."

Meanwhile, Jason paced the halls, grimacing in pain. He swallowed a couple more tablets for his headache.

"We can do this later," Mortyiene whispered.

"No we cannot," he whispered back. "From what you told me, I believe they are planning something big."

Rosliniah returned shortly with four peacekeepers. "You remember Chesmue and Elifelet," she said, pointing to two of the officers. "This is Desi and Sahora. Sahora is our medic in case someone gets injured."

Jason nodded his greeting. "We are going to execute an arrest warrant. Her name is Adelaydah Clayton and she has killed, or caused to be killed, ten people that we know of. She is considered very dangerous, so we will use enchanted cuffs to suppress her magic."

Desi shifted nervously, and closed her fingers around the hilt of her sword.

"We must take her alive, if possible," Jason continued, passing out an enchanted picture of Adelaydah.

Rosliniah glanced at the picture and handed it to Elifelet. She stepped forward and stood in front of the group of peacekeepers. "That means our main job is to keep the Investigator and the Agent alive. The suspect must stand trial. Limit the use of deadly force to emergencies."

With one last look at the assembled peacekeepers, Jason turned on heal and strode toward the student dorms, and Adelaydah's room.

Arriving at her room, he knocked on her door and shouted.

"Adelaydah open up, LBI." No answer. He stepped back, motioning for the armored peacekeepers to get closer, and murmured a spell to open locks. *"Olenhjau lojmnunlool lenJason nolmun"*

A small bolt of energy jumped from Jason's finger to the door, and the locking mechanism flared light blue and clicked open. The armored peacekeepers proceeded the investigators into the room, searching the wardrobe and bathroom. "Clear," they called, indicating it was safe for Jason and Mortyiene.

They entered the room and found a drained and dissected body of a library cat lay in an inscribed circle on the desk.

Edwardynah jumped onto the desk and sniffed the cat. She sat on her haunches and regarded Jason. "That's Chloe, she was from the illusionists section." She lashed her tail back and forth in anger.

Jason's hands trembled as he covered the tiny body with a cloth. "Shax requires dissected remains, does he not?" he asked Mortyiene.

Mortyiene frowned, staring down at the small lump under the cloth. "Yes, I believe he does. It looks like she was offering up cats for sacrifice."

Jason started rummaging through the papers on her desk. He picked up several notebooks and leafed through them, then he passed one to Mortyiene. "Look at this. She keeps mentioning Shax, but it is written in a language I am not familiar with."

Mortyiene took the book from his out-stretched hand. "That is because it is written in Draconic. It does name the demon she summoned. From the looks of this, it is a journal she had been keeping. She was researching a way to dismiss him and found a way. She is planning to make the sacrifice in the thaumaturgy section of The Library--a human sacrifice."

Jason looked through her notes and spells, it was only the one notebook on her thaumaturgical studies he couldn't read. "We need to stop her. Any idea of when this will happen?"

"She says that the circle has already been prepared in the

thaumaturgy section. She will perform the ritual today."

A quick glance through her notes revealed that Adelaydah had wandered in the forest outside of Pegasus Cove and had found a small temple to Aeverix, the god of chaos. The priest there told her she could find her revenge by making a deal with someone more powerful than herself.

As Jason listened to Mortyiene read through the notebooks his eyes filled with tears. It told of Adelaydah's pain at watching the woman die, knowing she could do nothing to help her. After the last person was killed, who was responsible for the death of the woman in Melegate, Adelaydah had tried to stop summoning the demon.

She noted that she was in the thaumaturgy section right now looking for the spell that would sever her connection to the abyss permanently. That she regretted her choices, and the truth of the demonic influence overwhelmed her.

Jason looked at Mortyiene, and said, "is there any way to get out of the contract?"

Mortyiene shook her head. "The only way is death. Even then your soul is lost."

Jason and Mortyiene, with the five peace keepers in tow, strode for the lifts to the thaumaturgy section.

At the door, Scarlet ran up to the group. "If you are going to bring in Adelaydah, I want to come."

Jason shook his head. "Sorry, but I cannot allow it. It could be extremely dangerous." He crossed his arms and glared at his childhood friend, his heart pounding in his chest. He knew how stubborn Scarlet was. She wouldn't listen, wouldn't stay behind.

Scarlet crossed her arms and jutted out her chin. "She has been my best friend since The Mountain. If anyone can get her to come in without a battle, it will be me."

Mortyiene looked at Jason. "She is right. She has the best chance of talking Adelaydah into giving up."

Jason frowned and then relented. "I do not like this, but I agree, provided you stay out of the way."

* * *

The lift doors opened onto the strangely clean but highly chaotic section of The Library. Deep black drapes adorned the walls softening the gray stone. Bloodiron wood tables rested on polished obsidian floors. Edwardynah moved through the stacks in stalking mode. The demonic cats of the section watched the group with blood red eyes. Spiders chittered near the ceiling in huge, grotesque, but strangely beautiful webs.

Chanting echoed from the center of the floor. Four voices joined as one. *"PoxShax xuixrix xax, Poxshax xhoxwrix xax, Poxshax xraxctrix xax xishx'x"*

The sound was not out of place. Rosliniah deployed the peace keepers in a circle around the spell casters. Jason, Scarlet, and Mortyiene tracked the chanting to its source.

"What are they chanting?" Jason's heart thumped in fear.

"I am not sure, but it sounds like they are summoning Shax. Come on. We still have time." Mortyiene's eyes flashed in barely contained excitement.

The first trap was triggered by Desi. Acid sprayed over her, and she screamed in pain. The viscous liquid covered her, melting away her skin. Sahora jumped to Desi's aide. He used an enchanted baliene, a first aid device, to scrape the ooze from her flesh. As Desi screamed, Sahora responded using spells, to stop the burning. Three spiders, spurred on by the triggered trap, dropped from the ceiling, shooting webs from their spinners and quickly covered the acid-soaked soldier with caustic silk.

Next to Desi, Sahora slashed at the webs. His knife disintegrated. Still the soldier screamed. Chesmue, Elifelet, and Rosliniah closed in and hacked at the spiders. A demonic cat launched itself at the wounded peacekeeper, its slashing claws extended.

"Zko ckotckeaz." Scarlet cried. A giant shard of ice flew

from her splayed hands and slammed into the twisted cat's body, flinging it away from the medic.

"Mouenfouelun" A light ray sprang from Jason's index finger and bored through a spider that was descending on its web. He dragged the wounded peacekeeper away from the stacks. The peacekeepers held up their shields to protect the librarian as he pulled their comrade away from the fray. More spiders dropped from the ceiling, circling the group. Shadows detached from the stacks, creeping closer.

"We need to move forward," Jason examined the soldier briefly. "She is dead. We cannot do anything for her."

Elifelet reached in his pocket and took out an enchanted iron cage. The black iron box was two inches squared. He put the box on the soldier's chest and activated the magic. It sprang into an iron cage that covered the dead soldier and latched itself onto the table. "That should keep them from getting in. The iron is enchanted to resist acids. Both natural and unnatural."

"We can't hold them off much longer Investigator," Rosliniah cleaved a spider with her sword.

"Why are they attacking?" Mortyiene asked. A sickly green ray streaked from her finger and hit a spider. The spider flared green for a second. It paused in its web, trembling.

"Don't know, Agent," Rosliniah yelled back, she slashed through a cat and two shadows. "The chanting seems to be enraging them."

Jason pressed forward with Scarlet and Mortyiene, flinging light bolt after light bolt, dispelling shadows and imps. The creatures advanced, pressing the peacekeepers who struggled to keep the magic users safe.

"Edwardynah. Get us out of here," Jason bellowed, looking for his cat.

"The thaumaturgists are down one floor." Mortyiene yelled into Jason's ear. "Illusionists are working. They are changing the direction the sound is coming from."

"More than one Illusionist?" Jason called back to Mortyiene.

Mortyiene tipped her head listening. "Yes. Kriston is helping Adelaydah. They are trying to get her out of The Library."

"Can you find the stairs?" Jason called to the cat.

Edwardynah streaked toward the thickest part of the battle. Cats, spiders and imps swarmed over the bookcases as the peacekeepers held their ground. "That way."

Jason groaned inwardly. He shot a few more light bolts while Scarlet and Mortyiene helped with the spell damage. "Captain, we need to go that way."

"Are you shitting me?" Rosliniah roared back. "Through that?"

"Yes, We have identified they are one floor down," Jason yelled. A light ray sprang from his index finger and burrowed into the eye of a demonic cat.

The captain saluted. She rallied the peacekeepers around her, forming a wall of steel. Behind which Jason, Mortyiene and Scarlet cast a continuous barrage of spells. Edwardynah stalked through the cats and spiders streaking unerringly toward a side door.

Scarlet stumbled, her hand grasping the stacks. Jason held her as they struggled against the onslaught. Breathing hard, sweat poured down his back. His wizard robes clung to his form. "How are you doing?" he yelled over the sounds of combat.

"Tired. We need to move." Scarlet's eyes danced with the inner fire of a sorceress.

"f'sazv zoweяvias ghuazdyas." Mortyiene summoned up a dark wave. It coalesced in front of the soldiers, pushing the creatures away. "Hold me up, I will see if I can push through to the door."

Jason supported her while Scarlet took over as rear guard, killing anything that attempted to sneak up behind them. They battled their way to the staircase.

They stumbled through the door, and slammed it behind them. *"Wallenun lojmuhau,"* A bolt of energy streaked through the key hole, locking the door with a librarians authority. Edwardynah

174

streaked down the stairs to the lower floor. "Follow her, she knows where we are going." Jason gasped, pounding down the stairs after his cat.

One floor down infernal heat blasted them. Deep heavy smoke filled the air and sent them coughing. Library cats stalked through the stacks. Visibility was reduced to mere inches.

The attacks ceased as they struggled through the smoke. The smell of brimstone choked them. As they drew nearer to the chanters, the language started eating at their souls. Fresh pain raced through his body adding to the pounding of his headache.

"Plug your ears," Jason yelled, as a couple of peacekeepers' ears started to bleed.

Jason felt his own ears bleeding. He stuffed in some cotton from his bag. "You have to be our ears," he shouted to Mortyiene and Scarlet. "What are they saying?"

"It sounds like they are almost done with the ritual. They are going to offer a sacrifice to appease their Lord. It is you." Mortyiene bellowed, so Jason could hear her through his earplugs.

"Me?" Jason roared. "Why me?"

"Not sure," Mortyiene replied. "I think it is because she likes you."

The group stumbled out of the stacks into an open area. The bloodiron wood tables were pushed to one side and three thaumaturgists formed a circle. In the center stood Adelaydah naked, covered in blood. The circle flared up and a talon stork like leg stepped out of a black and red swirling portal. Two more legs, followed by a massive body, nearly twenty feet tall, with the dove like head slid out of a red and black swirling portal. It stood over Adelaydah and molested her with an evil scalpel. Blood gushed between her legs as the hideous thing slid the scalpel in and out.

"Adelaydah," Scarlet screamed.

Adelaydah opened her eyes and stared at Scarlet. "No, you cannot be here. I told you to stay away."

"How could she?" Jason shouted. "You were her best friend.

She wanted to help you. Would you kill her to satisfy your lust? We know what happened. Why you did the things you did. Come in, give yourself up. We will make sure you are treated fairly."

The massive demon watched without blinking, his dove head moving back and forth. He whispered in his demonic language. *"Xoux xacxixizx'x ix axxzxaxre'x"*

"No!" Adelaydah screamed. "Not her."

The demon lord reared back, sword in hand, and flung it at Scarlet.

Adelaydah jumped into the path of the whirling blade, as the peacekeepers closed in around Scarlet. The blade sliced lengthwise through Adelaydah, and she fell to the floor cut cleanly into two pieces. The monstrous figure threw back his head in exalted triumph. With an ear splitting cry he summoned a bolt of fire.

"Get back!" Mortyiene screamed as she dove for cover, pulling Jason with her.

Scarlet stood in the center, rooted to the spot as she stared at Adelaydah's bloody body. The demon's flame roared toward her. Numbly she cast her shields. The abyssal flame flowed around her as her element, of fire, could not touch her. Fueled by the grief from the death of her friend, she raised her hands and started a chant. *"Cok cotzakeaz ok zko acd katzek tzis kezkg ok eck ckogk tzk kazkc."*

Scarlet flared with ice. It flowed through her body turning her limbs blue. Above her, plumbing burst, as she called upon every drop of water for three floors. A huge ice pillar encased the center of the circle, including the other three thaumaturgists. Its icy might focused on Shax's black figure.

The demon screamed as the spelled ice shattered into him. Even with earplugs, the party fell to its knees. Around them an inferno raged as books caught fire. The peacekeepers dropped their swords to the ground, and clamped their hands over their ears, screaming.

With an explosive ball of fire, Shax was pulled back into his world.

The stacks were a blazing inferno. The smell of cooking flesh and sulfur filled the air. The three remaining thaumaturgists were statues of ice dripping water.

Mortyiene grabbed Jason's hand, as Scarlet collapsed to the floor. "We have got to get out of here," she yelled. "before the fire suppression spells kick in."

Jason staggered toward Scarlet's prone form. He motioned for the peacekeepers to grab the girl. Elifelet flung her over his shoulder in a fireman's carry.

"Can we make it without Scarlet?" Jason called to the peacekeepers.

"Not sure, librarian," Rosliniah shouted, thrusting her way through the burning stacks. Books exploded around them and shelves crashed to the floor in showers of sparks.

"Edwardynah. Get us out of here," Jason demanded.

"Follow me." She streaked down an open area away from the fire.

"This way," he yelled to the guards.

"Librarian! That is the way we came in," Rosliniah yelled back, pointing the opposite direction.

"It is blocked," Jason roared. Another massive book case crashed in front of them. Books tumbled down in a shower of sparks. "We are cut off from the lifts. Edwardynah--follow her."

The feline darted out from behind a book case and ran down a side aisle. The peacekeepers, spying the cat, followed her. Jason followed, trusting Edwardynah to find the way out. He noticed, for the first time, he was not sneezing.

The cat streaked down the main aisle, past the thawing bodies of the three thaumaturgists and Adelaydah's bisected, blood-drenched form. Around them the fire roared, sucking oxygen from the air, making it difficult to breathe.

"Get down low," Edwardynah growled.

Jason roared the instructions to the others. They remained

crouched, as they ran to the staircase, which had become a chimney. The hand rails were ablaze. The demonic heat had spread throughout the whole floor of The Library. Jason recognized the area as the one closest to the necromancy section.

Edwardynah shot through the flaming bookcases toward the black iron-bound door that separated the thaumaturgy and necromancy sections. Around her, imps and cats rushed forward to attack the party. But the smoke and smells made it hard for them to track. Above their heads webs burned. Charred spiders fell to the floor around them.

The door to the necromancy section swung open on its own accord. Edwardynah bolted through it to the dusty rows of bookcases behind it.

Jason, Mortyiene, and the peacekeepers carrying Scarlet's unconscious, form dove through the open door. Behind them streamed a line of imps, cats, and shadows summoned from the abyss by the banishment of the abyssal lord. Jason turned to face them.

"No!" screamed Mortyiene. "Bli has sent us help. Get back. Sometimes they forget who you are."

Jason turned as the stream of undead melted out of the shadows. Skeleton's eyes glowed red in empty sockets showing that Bli was watching through them. The two armies clashed together. The unearthly screams of the undead mingled with the unholy screams of the abyss.

Black blood soaked the floor. The smell of brimstone filled the air. Jason and his companions pushed their way back further from the fighting. Edwardynah melted into the shadows. Jason, Mortyiene, Scarlet and the peacekeepers backed away from the dubious safety of the undead army.

Bli stood in front of the lift to the main floor awaiting them. "Did you find the killer?"

Scarlet, regaining consciousness, began to sob.

Jason glared at him and nodded.

"Then I take it Rhyann is free to go?" Bli hissed, his voice sending shivers down Jason's spine.

"Yes. She is, Librarian Bli," Jason emphasized the word Librarian.

Bli turned his skeletal face to Jason. "I would not have thought you could put aside your own feelings and allow her to go free."

Jason sighed. He held up his left hand, showing the white gold bracelet. "I am the Investigator for the LBI. My job is to find the truth."

"Even, apparently, when the truth brings you great pain." A plaintive note touched Bli's centuries old voice.

Jason ordered the peacekeepers to take Scarlet to the hospital wing. Behind the closed doors he heard a whoosh and a loud popping sound--The fire suppression system removed the air from the burning areas, and suffocated the flames.

"Captain, when it is safe, go down and retrieve the bodies. Now that they are all dead, the floor should be peaceful again," Jason said to Rosliniah. He felt dirty. The ash was working its way under his skin.

Rosliniah saluted him joined the peacekeepers as they took Scarlet to the hospital.

"Librarian, I have no wish to tarry in your domain. You have the thanks of the bureau for your assistance." Jason paused and turned back to the liche before leaving. "And my own thanks as well."

Jason entered the lift and pushed the button for the wizardry floor. He noticed that Edwardynah got on with him. He looked down at her and smiled. "Now I know what you are good for."

The cat twitched her tail and said nothing.

Chapter 13

Jason knocked on the hospital door, and heard Scarlet's voice invite him in. She was pale and drawn, propped up on pillows with her breakfast on the tray table

"It is good to see you awake," he said, sinking into a chair and pulling it closer to her bed. "We were a bit worried about you after you passed out from that spell you cast."

"I did not think I had it in me," she said through her a bite of her breakfast. "What happened to Adelaydah?"

"They waited for the fire to die down. By that time all of the bodies had been destroyed."

"And that priest outside of Pegasus Cove? What happened to him?" Scarlet mumbled through a mouthful of porridge.

"The LBI sent word to Pegasus Cove that he was there. They found his sanctuary and brought him to swift justice. It appears that Adelaydah was not the only one tricked by him."

Scarlet looked down. She pushed the last of her breakfast away.

Jason handed her the military records from Pegasus Cove that detailed the encounter and what had happened. "Adelaydah watched a woman of her village get gang-raped until she died. That tipped her over the edge. She reported them and they were all, including LaFlora, who had tried to stop them, discharged without honor. LaFlora was discharged for covering it up."

Scarlet's hands trembled as she read the report. Her eyes misted in tears as she glanced over the military records sent to Jason from Pegasus Cove.

"You see," Jason continued, "thaumaturgy is a parasite. It piggy backs onto other magical schools. Once you start using the syntax it works its way into your vocabulary, and soon you are using it without realizing it. After LaFlora died, Adelaydah tried to find another suitable sacrifice. One whose soul the demon wanted. She was hoping for me, but Shax, the demon she summoned, chose you instead."

"So she sacrificed herself to save me. To keep me from being his pawn." Scarlet's eyes were wet with tears.

Jason nodded. "The thaumaturgy librarian just got in the way, and was going to reveal who she was. She had to kill him. Shang, Yule, and LaFlora were the last of the soldiers directly involved with the death. Apparently that demon loved disease. With his help, she was able to mutate a strain of Bayou Malaria and infect a couple of the soldiers. By use of her illusions, she made it appear that a vampire killed the others. She opened her channel the first day here, which allowed her to craft illusions, disguising the demon to look like Rhyann specifically."

"Any reason why they attacked that woman?" Scarlet asked.

"When they got to Melagate, Rhyann had summoned several allies, including human thralls. A woman fled from the soldiers, and no one else in the village was alive they could see, so they assumed she was working for Rhyann. So they trapped and raped her. Unfortunately it was in front of the church of Ishkatar. Adelaydah saw the whole thing. Afterwards she reported it to LaFlora's commanding officer. LaFlora tried to stop the men from raping by ordering them to stand down. They were so caught up in their blood lust they did not hear the order. LaFlora was not aware that there were witnesses and tried to cover up what the soldiers had done. The seven of them were going to be court-martialed. Adelaydah was so traumatized, not only from the attack by the Vampiress but also from witnessing the rape, she came across as vengeful and disturbed. Her testimony was clouded with confusion. The army discharged the seven men and LaFlora without honor for the crime, and LaFlora for covering it up"

"And they were allowed to live in Pegasus Cove, so when Adelaydah came to live with my family she saw them and her hatred grew," Scarlet concluded.

"Yes, and she would ride outside of the city to get away and think. It was during these times that she stumbled upon the sanctuary of Aeverix. The priest of that temple taught her a means to exact vengeance."

"And that is how she started studying thaumaturgy." Scarlet finished his statement.

"She was also able to cast more powerful spells earlier on. Do you remember the first morning she was here she complained of a headache. It turns out she snuck into the Mana Chamber when no one was there and opened her channels before she was fully trained for the next level. The demon had encouraged her to do that so her power would be greater. Because of her more complex syntax she was able to more fully summon him to destroy Yule and LaFlora, and disguise him to look like Rhyann. However, she was not able to recreate the coagulum enzyme. That is how we were able to prove that Rhyann was not responsible for their deaths."

Scarlet burst out in tears and pushed away her tray table. "Why did she not tell me she was so angry? I would have helped."

Jason got up and hugged his friend. "I do not know. Whatever her reasons, I am sure it was to protect you. She was truly not expecting you to be with us when we went to arrest her. Shax's deal was to take the one that was most important to her, hence he would take you. She sacrificed herself at the end to protect you."

He held her until her body stopped shaking stroking her fiery hair as she sobbed in his arms. Finally, he got up and looked at her tear-streaked face.

"The Diagnostician said you could leave today. Let us meet for dinner at Sky Village Inn. You and Boris will be leaving soon. The Library is open again. I would like to see you one more time. But I have to go. I need to write a report of what happened and close the case."

Scarlet nodded and wiped her eyes dry. Jason got up and left the room, heading back to his office.

* * *

Jason and Mortyiene were in his office working on their reports, when there was a knock on the door.

Edwardynah looked up from her perch on Jason's desk and sniffed.

He got up and opened the door. Sarad and two of his men stood, Their hands clasped before them and adorned in the deep red robes of the nomads. Jason greeted them and ushered them to the sitting room.

"Investigator Jason," Sarad said, bowing low over his hands. "We wish to thank you for discovering who was behind the plague. Tell me sir, what happened?"

Jason sat on the chair and crossed his legs. "Your desert should be back to normal now that we have vanquished Shax. This is what happened."

"Shax was working through several conduits, and had his own agenda. We suppose he wished to take over The Library. Though Adelaydah gave him his initial foot-hold, once he was established in this world he set his sights on controlling The Library. That meant disrupting desert life so much that you and your people would be forced to attack for water and resources."

"It was because of Shax that the weather was disrupted and the wells were going dry. When Adelaydah entered the desert, Shax was able to take a much more direct hand. He mutated some desert scorpions, and, with Adelaydah's help, called them to attack the party. Adelaydah thought it was to get rid of Shang. However, Shax wanted Shang dead by, what appeared to be, a change in desert life. He knew you would demand resources, and that your honor would insist that you attack The Library. What he did not count on, was your honor would also demand you work with The Library to find out who was behind the attacks."

"So this disruption of my people was related to a massacre on the other side of the world?" Sarad looked stunned.

"Sadly, yes. Although the machinations of the abyss do transcend human squabbles. Shax would have wanted The Library eons before Adelaydah came along. Adelaydah just provided him with the conduit needed to come and wreak havoc on you."

"Jason." Sarad stood and bowed low over his hands once again. "You have proven yourself to be honorable and fair in this. My thanks for not holding my people accountable for the raid on Sky Village. We deeply regret the hasty attack, and will make amends for the deaths we have caused."

"That will please the people of Sky Village. I am glad we could put hostilities behind us and live as brothers in the desert. I believe the administrator has allowed you use of the great oasis for your herds until the wells refill. You are welcome among us."

Sarad and his tribesmen bowed low once more and left the room.

Jason turned to Mortyiene. "Let us finish up the paperwork. I want to celebrate."

* * *

Jason was reading a book when a knock on the door signaled that he had company. "Come in," he called.

Edwardynah was asleep on the sofa. He still sneezed when she was around, but now he didn't complain about it. The door opened allowing Mortyiene and Rhyann stride in.

Rhyann glided forward and held out a cool hand. "I wanted to thank you Investigator, for proving I was not responsible for those deaths."

Jason stood and stared down at her hand, coldly refusing to shake it. "But you are responsible for those deaths, only you did not commit the murders. They were a direct result of your actions and your attack on Melegate. If you had not destroyed that village the door would not have been open to allow Shax access to Adelaydah's heart, and she would not have been driven to kill."

Rhyann glared at Jason coldly. "I came to express my thanks-- and you insult me," she hissed.

"I would do more than that, if I was able. I would wrap you up with a big bow and send you back to Pegasus Cove for them to stake you out to greet the sun. But, as it stands, I am the Investigator for The Library. Even though your actions nearly destroyed the tentative peace, you remain innocent of murder."

"Jason," Mortyiene gasped. "She came here to express her gratitude."

"And I choose not to accept her gratitude. I choose to speak the truth. Though she is not guilty of those murders, she is responsible. The only thing that keeps me from holding her accountable is that acts of war are not admissible. I will thank her to leave The Library, and soon, before her presence stirs up more trouble. Many in Sky Village still hold her accountable. The sooner she leaves the more thorough the peace will be."

Rhyann drew herself up and locked her gaze with Jason. He could feel warmth and safety in those eyes. He blinked once and shook himself. "Mesmerizing a librarian is also against the law," he murmured under his breath, fighting to keep his wits about him.

"Rhyann," Mortyiene hissed.

The feeling of warmth and safety vanished, as Rhyann pulled her gaze from Jason's eyes.

"Librarian, you had best hope I never get hold of you away from The Library. I do not often show gratitude, but I did today."

"And I did not accept it. I bid you a good night and wish you a speedy journey back home." With that he returned to his chair and picked up his book, as Mortyiene and Rhyann left his rooms.

Edwardynah looked up at him and rubbed against his arm.

"You did well Jason," she purred.

"Maybe, but I doubt if I made a friend." He absently stroked her soft fur and sneezed a couple of times.

"Well, you are the Investigator. No other librarian can move between the different stacks with your authority. It is better you keep your beliefs firmly in place, as you will need all of your internal strength about you for the rest of your life."

Jason laughed and stroked his cat once more before returning to his book. Edwardynah jumped down and curled up on one of the chairs, purring softly.

Chapter 14

The thaumaturgy section had been rebuilt for several weeks now. Jason and Mortyiene stayed at the library sharing an office. Boris and Scarlet had returned to Pegasus Cove. Lucero had returned to Eversphere.

Mortyiene's family and the Uver were unhappy that Mortyiene would not be coming back, but she had accepted the position of agent. Another desk was brought into Jason's office for her to use. She retained her rooms and even contacted the owner of Bina and bought her for a fair amount.

Jason was asleep in his bed, as the fire embers died in the fireplace. Dreams, once again, plagued him. Something that had not happened since he journeyed to The Library.

One particularly vivid dream rose up before his sleeping eyes. He could see Adelaydah being tortured in a vast hall. Night after night she would be dissected alive. Minions would revel in her viscera as she screamed out in torment. Her blood was now black with age. Jason jerked awake, sitting up in his bed, and rubbing his eyes

A transparent figure of an apparition stood at the foot of his bed. Adelaydah, now a tormented spirit, screamed silently. He pinched himself to see if he was awake. Finally he heard her voice echoing across the planes.

"Help me Jason," she cried.

He stared at the ghost and it faded. Oh crap, he thought as he flopped back in his bed.

The End

28324561R00119

Made in the USA
Charleston, SC
08 April 2014